I0616461

ISBN: 0692545514
ISBN-13: 978-0692545515

To my father Wilson,

For encouraging me to continue to write, regardless of whether or not people will like my stories or think they're funny. I will always miss your wisdom and humor, but the memories of your laughter will always reside in my heart.

# STORIES

noonelovesyou.com

No One Will Love You As Much As I Never Did

## A SOCIABLE SUICIDE

It was a typical day at the office, and I was tending to my usual responsibilities. I've always been a meticulous worker. This morning, however, I felt an incredible sense of unease. In the darkest, most forgotten corner of my brain, a match was struck, and a feeling I would often visit fondly in my youth suddenly reemerged after years of absence. I couldn't quite wrap my head around it. I've always hated the phrase, 'wrap my head around it.' Don't even get me started.

The feeling hit me as I was typing my tenth email to Marvis that morning, the mailroom attendant who screwed up the shipment that was essential for the expo occurring in Durham that day. It was nowhere to be found. You may be wondering what this essential shipment was. It was a shipment of posters on foam core. They needed to arrive in Durham on time or else the world would burn to ashes – from Hong Kong to Sydney, Paris to Quito, it would all crumble if the posters didn't arrive. It was more important than curing cancer to everyone at my office.

The posters didn't arrive; meaning Rome was beginning to burn. The match's flame in my brain was rising. I got the blame for the missing posters, so I received a tongue lashing from my boss – who should be the last person to reprimand me, with me knowing his darkest secrets. It would be far too embarrassing for me to write here or ever reveal to anyone else. I'll take those secrets with me to the grave. Anyway, my boss Todd came into my office to lash me with that tongue of his.

"Johnson, you son of a bitch. Assume to position, you're going to get a lashing, you son of a bitch," he said.

I forgot to mention that Todd likes for people he's about to give a verbal lashing to, to stand with their backs facing him as if he's actually lashing you with his tongue, and you just take it – a truly degrading procedure, I know, but again, I have secrets about him. It's also worth noting that he likes to excessively use the phrase 'son of a bitch.'

I stood with my back to him, spread my legs, and rested my palms in front of my body, on my desk.

"Yes, that's it, stand with those butt cheeks high in the air, you sorry, good for nothing son of a bitch. How loud did your mother howl when she had to get that bulbous head of yours out of her dusty vagina, you son of a bitch? You know that shipment had to arrive in Durham today. You know what, though, Johnson?"

"No, what, sir?"

"You're a son of a bitch."

It would take the next 'son of a bitch' to make me crack.

"Get back to work. You really messed up, but I suppose mistakes happen. I'm sure you'll make sure to follow closely with shipping next time some important items need to arrive to their destinations."

"May I stop standing like this, sir?"

"Oh, of course, and please, call me Todd."

"Thanks, Todd, I'll make sure this will never happen again."

"You betcha. See you later, you son of a bitch," he said as he slapped my buttocks.

I'm not sure whether it was a snap in my brain or the sound of someone snapping a pencil outside of my office, but there was a snap, nonetheless.

"That's it. That's enough of it. You know what, I need to make an announcement," I said and stormed out of my office, shoved Todd aside, and stood in the middle of a row of cubicles. I cleared my throat, rolled both my hands into fists, and allowed the words to naturally come out as they were intended to.

"Hello, may I have everyone's attention? As most of you know, I've been with this company for almost six years. While this may come as a surprise, life could be pretty *shocking* at times, but that's what makes it so darn *electrifying*."

No one laughed at my pun.

"Anyway, I am pleased to announce that I, Johnson to most of you, will kill myself this coming Friday at five o'clock. It sucks that it's only Monday and you have to wait until the end of the week, but you know what, I'll make my office available to any of you who would like to come in and say 'what's up,' want to 'hang loose,' or something like that from here on to the end. Do you have any questions?"

Fitzgerald raised his hand.

"Yes, you, Fitzgerald!"

"Yeah, how are you going to do it?" He asked.

"Oh, I don't know, possibly slit my wrists, drink rat poison, swallow a ton of pills —"

"That's the coward's way out..." Hernandez interrupted.

"Yeah, I suppose you're right, Hernandez. That would be the coward's way to do it. How about I jump in front of a subway car?"

"Yeah, that's better..." Hernandez said.

"Any other questions?" I asked.

"Are you going to leave a will? I mean, you're not married," Jenkins asked.

"Yes, Jenkins, you're right on that, too. I will email Todd my will and CC you all. How does that sound?" I said.

"Yeah, send us an all-hands email. That would be pretty cool to have. I'll save it in my personal files, you know," Jenkins added.

"I know and appreciate that, Jenkins. Thank you."

"No problem. You know you were always my boy."

"Always."

Jenkins blushed after I said that to him.

"Any other questions? Yes, you, Ferrigno."

"When you say five o'clock on Friday, do you mean in the morning or in the afternoon?" Ferrigno asked.

"Sorry I didn't clarify. For your convenience, I'll do it at five o'clock in the *afternoon*. I wouldn't want to inconvenience you by having to come in at five in the morning. That'd just be preposterous," I said.

"Oh, ok. Thanks for being accommodating," Ferrigno said.

"I have a question," Todd said.

"Shoot, Todd. No, I'm just kidding, I'll do the shooting myself," I said. The office burst into laughter after I said that.

"That's very funny, Johnson," Todd said while wiping the tears from his eyes after laughing so hard. "Will you want an office party for your impromptu suicide?"

"I wouldn't mind that, Todd, but please acknowledge that this technically isn't an impromptu suicide since I won't be doing it right now, so I'd make sure you get the facts straight before you send out that mass email about the party. You don't want to look like a boob, you know."

"Yeah, you're right, you son of a bitch, I didn't think about that. Thanks, Johnson!"

"Alright, well, I'll be in my office if anyone wants to come in, chat, ask any other questions, or just throw the old pigskin around."

"I want to say one more thing, Johnson," Todd said. "I hereby proclaim that after your very sociable suicide, I will posthumously promote you to vice president of this department. I will use this stapler to represent you while you're gone." He showed everyone a stapler he pulled off of Cunningham's desk.

"While I'm gone? I'm not coming back, Todd. Don't you mean *from that point on?*"

"Oh, that's right. What will I do without you?"

"I guess you'll have to see."

"That's the spirit, you son of a bitch!"

I went back into my office, and the ball started rolling on my suicide party. I received a call from the CEO of the company. News sure did travel fast.

"Hi, this is Johnson," I answered.

"Johnson, this is Roddick Harrison. I wanted to congratulate you on your magnificent announcement. May you have a delightful week!"

"Thanks so much, Roddick! I'm so glad you've already heard the news! Are you flying out for my farewell party?"

"I'd love to! I will be there via video conference. Do you think that since I'm the CEO, that you could tell me how you're going to do it?"

"I'm going to have to get back to you on that one, Roddick. Is inhaling my car's exhaust in my garage an easy way out?"

"Too easy. You would want to do it in a way that leaves a lot of blood. You want the best suicide possible. Remember, son, the bigger the death, the bigger the cheers. Do you want to be remembered for having the lamest suicide ever?"

"I see your point, Roddick. You're a wise man beyond your years."

"Hey, I'm not the CEO for nothing. So, how do you think you'll do it now that you know you want to make it big?"

"Hmmm...Promise you won't reveal the big secret?"

"Let's just say that I'm listening to a particular Go-Go's song right now, and it's not *Vacation*."

"Your lips better stay sealed, you big bastard! No, but seriously, I don't know. Since I'm doing it at work, maybe it'll be something that everyone in the building could enjoy, not just people on this floor. I'm thinking maybe I'll just throw myself out the forty-fifth floor window."

"That's the spirit, Johnson! I fully support that method. I'll make sure the boys are on the ground level to clean up the mess. I have a very important meeting I need to go to, so I'll let you go for now. If I remember to, I'll video conference in to your suicide party. Also, please consider me being present when your blood stains the walls. See what I'm getting at?"

"I read you loud and clear, Roddick. Thanks so much, and have a great day."

When I left my office for lunch, I was greeted one hand clap, then two hand claps, and then three hand claps, and then I heard the whole floor clapping.

"You the man, Johnson," Biggs said.

"Who else would it be?" I said as I shrugged my shoulders with a smirk on my face.

While at lunch, I stopped by the pizzeria across the street. I told the Mexican cashier I was going to kill myself.

"Voy a suicidarme," I said to him.

"Really, you're going to kill yourself?" He said. "That's awesome! You going to do it the gross way or the easy way?"

"No sé todavía. Tal vez me lanzo fuera del edificio."

"Oh, really? That should be awesome. When and what time?"

"Después de trabajo el viernes."

"You making a will? Leaving anything for me? Come on, man, I put on that extra cheese for you all the time."

"Te voy a dejar mi coche."

"Really? Oh, wow, thanks so much!"

"De nada."

He gave me my slices with extra cheese, and it was the tastiest lunch I ever had. I stayed at the pizzeria for a while and chatted with the employees about summer camp memories. I went back to the office at four fifty-eight. I was hoping to leave at that time.

"Hey, Todd, mind if I leave a little early?"

"I don't know, two minutes? Well, I guess you could. I mean, you are killing yourself anyway. You know what, you could have tomorrow off. Don't tell the other guys this or else they'll kill me!"

"Hey, don't you worry, I won't tell anyone. I'm the only one dying this week! But, assure them I haven't done it so they don't start to worry!"

"Oh, don't *you* worry, Johnson!"

I called my mother when I got home to tell her the news.

"Really?" She asked incredulously.

"Yes, I told the guy at the pizzeria *and* the CEO of my company how I'd do it."

"Well, don't you forget to leave me in the will. Hey, are you going to leave a note?"

I hadn't thought of a note, actually. I didn't really feel the need to write one.

"I don't know yet. I'll see if I feel like it later on," I said.

I stayed in bed for most of the next day. I wanted to be at one with myself. After all, it was one of the last times I was going to have *me* time before I committed suicide. I think I'd rather keep that time for myself, and not for your prying eyes. I mean, after all, I am being very candid with my suicide.

Wednesday was the day to finalize my projects and close any pending ones. I arrived to the office to find my office door decorated like a high school locker. It was covered in pink wrapping with yellow, blue, and red balloons. Pictures of me were pasted on it. Some creative drawings complemented the pictures, like what I would look like if I were an iguana, a raspberry, and my favorite: what I would look like if I were gay.

Todd drew a penis next to my mouth and wrote, "Eat that, you son of a bitch! <3 <3 143 143!"

"Guys, you didn't have to!" I said. The emotions were high, and I was getting teary-eyed.

"Hey," Hernandez said as he patted and grabbed my right shoulder. "We insist."

"Thanks, man," I said. "Now, if you'll excuse me, I have a ton of work I need to finish up. I'm going to keep my door closed. Don't you worry, though, I'll be breathing behind it."

"You'd better be, you son of a bitch. I don't want you dying on us until Friday, five p.m.!" Todd said.

"That's the day after tomorrow! I really need to do a lot before then," I said.

I found post-it notes all over my desk.

Some post-it notes read: *Way to go, Johnson!; Top Ace!; Number One!; You're still the man – Biggs.*

"Those guys, they're so sweet," I whispered to myself.

I had a lot to do, so I stayed in my office and was on the phone closing my deals. Most of my clients congratulated me on the good news, and it was posted on the office memo that went around. I was receiving accolades from all over! My day flew by. It was five-on-the-dot when I looked at my watch. Boy, oh, boy, time did fly faster than it usually did, it seemed.

I passed out on my couch as soon as I got home. When I woke up, it was seven in the morning! I was going to be late to the office!

Everyone was concerned when I finally got there. My colleagues thought I killed myself the night before, potentially putting a buzzkill on their weekend. I didn't want to do that to them.

"We thought we lost you, Johnson. You gotta stick around for one more day!" Someone said.

"Johnson, I want to know how you're going to do it. If it's going to be messy and include blood, I want the blood for my cubicle," someone else said.

"Johnson, I want to breathe your dead blood," someone I don't remember not saying something else said.

My party was that afternoon. It was a three-hour event. I passed the torch to the stapler that would replace me. Todd spoke about virtue, devotion, and efficiency, while the shy stapler said nothing. Roddick Harrison never showed up on video conference. He was probably busy doing other important things, which is understandable.

The party consisted of a cooler full of Coronitas, some bags of pretzels, and a third of a turkey sandwich someone didn't get a chance to finish at lunch. In case you're wondering, the sandwich was delicious!

A speech was asked out of me.

I wanted to be succinct, so I simply said, "Can't wait 'til tomorrow!"

The room erupted after I said that. People started cheering, raising the roof, and pounding their chests against the nearest person they could find.

After the ceremony, a visibly drunk Todd exclaimed, "You bastards! Tomorrow's going to be a huge day! You could all go home early, you son of a bitch!"

"Todd, there are more than one of us here, so you should say, 'you sons of bitches!'"

"Damn it, Johnson, you were always right about things like this! Now, get out of here and don't forget to come back tomorrow, you son of a bitch. But, wait! Before we all go, how are you going to do it?"

"I'm glad you reminded me, Todd! I'm going to jump out of the forty-fifth floor window. That shouldn't disappoint any of you, right?"

The reaction to my news was the same one I received after I gave my speech: everyone started cheering, raising the roof, and pounding their chests against the nearest person they could find. Fitzgerald even poured beer on me.

"Take this to the grave with you, ya' big lug," he said as he poured the Coronita on me, reminiscent of a football coach being drenched with a cooler full of ice after winning the big game.

When I got home, I debated on writing a note. I decided not to.

While in bed, my brain asked a strange question.

"Why?" My brain asked.

"It's what I've always wanted to do," I said in response.

"Why?" It asked again.

"I don't know. Stop being so paranoid!"

"Ok, I guess you're right," it said in response, and we both went to sleep.

The next day at the office was bizarre after all the buildup that went into it. People were performing their same routines. Phone calls and deliveries were being made, faxes were being sent, Todd was giving Rivera a tongue lashing in the style he liked. It was all too boring, considering the day's circumstances.

I had nothing to do because I had finalized my projects. I didn't have an office anymore because the stapler occupied it. I was forced to sit on the floor, next to Todd's office. No one took notice of me. No one even looked in my direction. It wasn't until Todd tripped over me when someone finally acknowledged my existence.

"Johnson, you son of a bitch, you're here? I didn't even see you. Say, it's almost four o'clock. You ready?"

"I am ready, but I don't want people missing out. I mean, I did tell everyone five o'clock."

"You're right. Come into my office, and shut the door behind you."

As I took a seat in Todd's office, he handed me what looked like a bandana.

"Here, wear this when you jump out of the window," he said to me.

"Why do you want me to wear it?"

"It belonged to me when I was your age, in your position. I once told myself I was going to commit a spectacular suicide like the one you're about to, but chickened out the last minute," he said and then closed his eyes. "I want to vicariously live through your suicide. I want to feel as if I'm along for the ride when you hit the pavement and your guts spew out against the first floor windows, you son of a bitch."

"Sure, Todd, of course, whatever you say," I said as I put the bandana in my pocket.

"I'm going to save some of the blood you leave behind in a vial and place it by the water cooler so everyone could remember you when they gossip around it."

"There would be no greater honor. Thank you so much, Todd."

"Hey, what are friends for? Get over here, you son of a bitch," Todd said as he got up and gave me a great, big bear hug. "I have bad news. Turns out Roddick Harrison won't be able to tune in to your suicide. I have the privilege of recording it for him, though."

"Todd, I would be honored if you did it."

"I know, Johnson, I know."

"Want a last meal?"

"Sure, what do you have?"

"It's half an M&M."

"Todd, I'm so grateful that you're sharing that with me. Thank you so much!"

"You're welcome, you son of a bitch."

He handed me the M&M piece, and it was the best I had ever eaten. Now that I think of it, I had the best of a lot of things that week.

"Mmmmmm. Now, that hit the spot!" I said.

"Well, I've got a lot of work to do here, and need to hop on a conference call, so I'm going to have to ask you to leave. I'll see you at five," Todd said, shooing me out of his office.

"Yeah, I'll see you at five."

I went back to waiting outside of Todd's office until it was showtime, five o'clock.

At precisely five p.m., a buzzer rang throughout the office.

"I just realized that I was never presented with a life insurance option," I said as soon as I heard the buzzer.

"You win some, you lose some," someone I didn't care about said.

"Yeah, he's right," Hernandez said.

"Yeah, you're right, Hernandez, and thank you for making me realize that," I said. "You do win some, and then you do certainly lose some. Anyway, enough of my jibber-jabber. What's everyone waiting for? Follow me!"

I ran towards the elevator, and everyone followed. We were seventeen floors away from my destined forty-fifth.

Everyone wanted to ride in the elevator with me, but I chose Todd, Hernandez, and Biggs. Todd recorded a video of me on his cell phone.

"Hey, Roddick, check out these lethal weapons," I said as I flexed for the cell phone camera.

When we reached the forty-fifth floor, I walked straight to the lobby window. The maintenance worker did us the favor of unlatching and opening it.

"Think you'll hear butterflies scream?" The maintenance worker asked me.

"Hey, I'm not telling," I said with a smirk on my face.

I pulled out the bandana Todd gave me and put it on my head. Todd saluted me with tears of joy when he saw me put it on.

Everyone formed a semicircle around me as I stood facing the sky, open breeze, and horizon. The ground below looked like a giant canvas that was missing a Pollock-esque splat. I needed to leave my mark on it.

"Johnson, any last words before you make greatness happen?" Todd asked.

"Yeah, I sent out that email will this morning from home, but I scheduled it to be sent at six-thirty, which means that most of you will have to wait until Monday because I know you won't want to stay late in the office on a Friday. Also, if I land on my face, free pizza for everyone at the pizzeria across the street!"

Everyone began to cheer and give each other high-fives.

"Well, gotta go!" I said, and with a swift lunge, I jumped off the forty-fifth floor window ledge. As I was airborne, the air screaming into my ears sounded like the most beautiful song I had never heard. I felt like I was flying with my fingertips until I hit the pavement. It was a magnificent death.

## EVERYTHING I LEARNED ABOUT BEING A MAN
## I LEARNED FROM CHARLIE FERRIGNO

The Random House Unabridged Dictionary defines "mentor" as *a wise and trusted counselor or teacher*. The Random House Unabridged Dictionary defines "hero" as *a man of distinguished courage or ability, admired for his brave deeds and noble qualities as well as a person who, in the opinion of others, has heroic qualities or has performed a heroic act and is regarded as a model or ideal.* Charlie Ferrigno is neither of those things by modern society's standards. He is often referred to more as a scumbag, douchebag, dirtbag, and various other bags. However, Charlie is not seen as any type of 'bag' to one person, his best friend Bobby – who happens to be eight years old. Almost anyone would have been bewildered by their friendship – as to why a grown man would be friends with a child. The answer to that question is that Charlie was what societal standards would refer to as a 'loser.' Bobby often went to Charlie's two hundred square-foot basement apartment to have his homework done for him. It was a self-esteem booster for Charlie to be regarded as vastly intelligent in the eyes of an eight-year-old. Charlie, out of the goodness of his heart, charged Bobby ten dollars to do his homework for three out of his six class subjects. That was, "The best deal in town, B-man," Charlie said.

"But I don't have the twenty dollars for you to do my homework for *all* my subjects. I'm swamped! I have to write a two-page story for reading class tomorrow, review questions for science, this work sheet with word problems for math, and the two questions Mrs. Harris gave us for social studies. Besides, it's only four subjects. Why are you charging me twenty dollars for four? I thought it was ten dollars for three. Shouldn't it be twenty dollars for six?" Bobby said.

"You know, your math teacher started fucking up my operation ever since she taught you word problems. Hey, it's still the best deal in town, don't you remember me saying that? I dare you to find someone who's willing to do this at a cheaper price. Go ahead, ask that guy Randolph who lives by the cemetery. First off, you'll be followed by the perverted ghost of Martin Garner. He's buried in the cemetery. Do you want to be haunted by a predator? It'll be gross. He'll be fondling your toys and doing who knows all over them while you're sleeping. You think it was bad when your dog Duke pissed in your toy chest? Trust me, Martin would do far worse. It makes me upset just thinking about it. And besides, Randolph can't have any more than a second grade education. I'm the only guy who's capable of doing this, B-man. So, what's it gonna be? You wanna flunk? Hey, it's not my ass. I passed the third grade – with flying colors, might I add. Look at me now…" Charlie said and then realized he lived in a studio apartment that was far from ideal – even in the eyes of an eight-year-old.

"I mean, look at me now, I'm so done with having to do homework of my own. I'm living large and stock up on as much ice cream as I want in my freezer. Look at all that ice cream, dude. I mean *look* at it," he said as he walked to the kitchen space and opened his freezer to find three Klondike bars.

"But, I only get a five-dollar allowance every week! I saved up for two weeks and paid you on Monday to do my phonics and handwriting homework! I don't have any more money," Bobby said.

"Alright, stop whining. Annoying much? I'll tell you what. Here's a plan that'll benefit the both of us," Charlie said as he started lifting a five-pound weight. "You're gonna have to go home while your father's asleep and take twenty dollars from his wallet. You're gonna to have to be on your tiptoes – just like a puma going after gazelle. Remember reading about that in your science textbook? Oh, that's right, you don't because I answered the review questions in the chapter about grassland animals. Where does he keep his wallet?"

"On top of his dresser."

"So, go in there, find his wallet, and take out a twenty. I doubt he'll even notice. If he wakes up, tell him you took a wrong turn and have to use the bathroom. You're at that age where kids still piss themselves, I think. He'll be so quick to get you out of his room that he'll forget he caught you stealing twenty dollars from him."

"Fine! But, I can't do it right now. This homework is due tomorrow! I can't take the money from him now!"

"Tough brake, B-man. But, I'll tell you what. I'm a nice guy with a heart mushier than the stale burrito behind my couch. I'll do three of the four subjects tonight, but I'll have to hold off on the fourth one until I get paid. Either you do the Social Studies homework yourself, get it all wrong, and get an F – or you hand it in a day late and get an A- instead of an A. The choice is yours, B-man. It's not *my* permanent record."

"That's so unfair!"

"I'm teaching you in two ways. One, you could review and learn the right answers once I fill them in for your class tomorrow. And two, you could view this as the first time you realized in your young life that life in general isn't fair. Sometimes you have to walk down the street to get milk from the corner store while cupping your nuts with your right hand. You'll never know when life's gonna come on by and try to kick 'em."

Bobby was confused by the metaphor, and was now afraid he'd be kicked in the groin the next time his mother asked him to go to the corner store to buy milk.

"Fine, I guess you're right," Bobby acquiesced. "I'll get you your twenty dollars tomorrow and take the lower grade."

"I knew you were growing into a smart boy. I don't negotiate with just anyone, you know. I always demand cash, upfront, before I lift a finger," Charlie said as if other children asked him to do their homework. "You're my main man, you're my guy. You're my bud to the end. I'll tell you what. While I get cracking with the two-pager, check out these dog fight DVD's I just bought. One of them has footage of two crazed Chihuahuas going at it. Check this, one of them sinks its teeth right through the other's eye. It's totally funny!"

"Yeah, put that in for me!"

"You got it, dude…"

Bobby got home at around seven o'clock. His mother greeted him as he walked into the kitchen through the back door.

"Bobby, you're home late. Why don't you go take a shower and do your homework, honey?" She said as she was preparing dinner.

"I already finished my homework at the after-school program."

"Oh, you did? That's nice, honey," she said, distracted. She didn't know Bobby had stopped going to the after-school program and started spending hours at Charlie's apartment.

"Why's dinner so late?" Bobby asked.

"It was a late day in the office. You know, you can't expect to have dinner ready for you every time you walk in through that door. Now, why don't you take that shower, honey, you smell like grandpa."

"Alright, mom," Bobby said as he walked upstairs. "Is Duke around?"

"Yes, dear."

"I don't want him peeing in my toy chest again," Bobby said, remembering the peeing incident Charlie had reminded him about earlier.

"That's nice, dear," Bobby's mother said, not paying attention.

During dinner, Bobby's mother and father were talking about their day at the table, but Bobby was distracted thinking about how he was going to sneak into their room and steal twenty dollars from his father's wallet. He was considering urinating himself to make his 'wrong turn to the bathroom' ruse more believable.

"Well Bobby?" His father asked, catching him off-guard.

"Well what, dad?"

"How was school today? Learn anything fun?"

Bobby started to think fast. He didn't pay an ounce of attention in any of his classes because he knew Charlie would bail him out with the homework. He heard a thing or two about Thomas Jefferson and the Boston Tea Party, and meshed them together with other tidbits he heard earlier that week. He put his improvisational skills to the test.

"Well, we learned that Thomas Jefferson threw an awesome tea party in Boston. It started when this guy Patrick Henry, I think, said 'Give me party or give me death,' and all these Indians came over on a boat with the tea. Paul Revere then got on a horse and started yelling at everyone in Boston that the British were coming to the party. They got to the party late, though. Some of the British soldiers brought alcohol to the party and got drunk, so they started shooting at some people, and that was then considered a Boston Massacre – probably because they were so drunk, because only like two people were killed."

"That's…interesting…" Bobby's father said. "What's your teacher's name again?"

"Mrs. Harris."

"Well, I think I should give Mrs. Harris a call tomorrow. Oh, shoot, I can't. I have two presentations in the morning and will be in meetings all day. Liz, how about you? Could you call to see what the meaning of this is?"

"I can't, John. I have four houses to show tomorrow. I have no time. I'm sure other students' parents call up about this. It's absurd. Are you making this up, Bobby? Did Mrs. Harris really teach you that? I understand trying to make history more fun for students, but this is ridiculous."

"Every word," Bobby said.

"This isn't good at all. I'll write myself a reminder on my phone to call your principal first thing tomorrow morning. In the meantime, you'll have to read your textbooks a little more closely," Bobby's father said. "Which reminds me. You will not believe what Thompson did today. He had the nerve to…"

Bobby's mind drifted off again. He looked at his father and thought he was nowhere near as cool as Charlie. He then wondered what kind of ice cream his father ate, and realized that his father didn't eat ice cream. He pictured himself as Charlie's son. He envisioned the two of them sitting on the floor, spread-eagle, eating Klondike bars, with Charlie saying, "You're dripping chocolate on the carpet, you fucking doof."

Later that evening after he went to bed, Bobby awoke and looked at his clock. It was 1:04 a.m. He thought it was the perfect time to execute the plan. He got up and tiptoed out of his room. He peeked out of his doorway to see if the coast was clear, and saw Duke asleep by the stairs and his parents' door ajar. He shimmied against the wall towards the bathroom. When he got there, he splashed toilet water on his pants. He figured it would be more believable to he wet himself with toilet water instead of water from the sink. Bobby continued to shimmy towards his parents' bedroom after he splashed water on his groin. He slipped into their room. His heart was pounding so fast that he was afraid the thumping would wake the both of them. He looked to the left of the bed, at his father's nightstand. On top of it was the wallet. He was certain there was a twenty-dollar bill in there. He tiptoed a little closer, reached, and got a hold of it. He had done it! His father then coughed. Bobby panicked and quickly opened the wallet. He took out the first bill he saw, put it in his pocket, threw the wallet, and heard his father exclaim, "BOBBY, WHAT THE HELL ARE YOU DOING?"

"Daddy, I peed my pants," Bobby immediately said.

"Oh, shit. Liz! Wake up, Liz. Bobby pissed his pants. Bobby pissed his pants!" His father yelled.

"Bobby pissed his pants?" Bobby's mother groggily said as she turned on the light on her nightstand to see what happened, and saw Bobby's wet spot. "Oh, Bobby, honey! You wet yourself? My poor baby!"

Bobby started to cry. "I'm *so* embarrassed!" He said with his arms stretched out towards his parents.

"Aww, pumpkin," his mother said.

"Verbally coddling him won't dry him! Go to the bathroom, Bobby, and change your pants! You need to get into the shower!" His father said.

"Wait! Before you do that," his mother said as she pulled open her nightstand drawer. "You have to stay like that. It's so adorable!"

She pulled out a camera and took a picture of Bobby looking pathetic as he stood crying, arms stretched out, with a wet spot on his groin.

"Liz! Are you kidding me? Bobby, go to the bathroom, NOW!" His father yelled.

Bobby ran into the bathroom and took the bill out of his pocket. He successfully took a twenty-dollar bill out of the wallet. He tossed it into the cabinet underneath the sink and took off his pants.

"Mom! Bring me a new pair of pants!" He yelled.

"He's eight years old. He still wets himself? Isn't he a little too old to be doing that? I'm concerned," Bobby's father said.

"What do you want to do about it? Want to call a therapist or something?" His mother asked.

"No, let's wait until he does it again. At least he didn't shit himself like your dad did a few weeks ago. That was disconcerting. I'm killing myself before I reach that age when I start doing that on a regular basis."

"You're such an asshole. You know my dad is epileptic. He's only fifty-seven years old," Bobby's mother responded as she got out of bed. "Now excuse me, I have to pass my son a new pair of pants, you mindless, despicable fuck."

Bobby stood nervously in the bathtub.

His mother walked in with latex gloves, tossed him a new pair of underwear and pants, picked up the wet pants and underwear, and threw them into a plastic bag.

"I need to throw this out. It'll reek in here if I put it somewhere," she said without being cognizant of the fact that it didn't smell like urine.

"Are you alright, honey?" She asked him. "Did you have a bad dream?"

"Yes, mommy, I did."

"It's alright, honey, it's alright. Want me to sleep in your bed with you?"

"No, it's ok. I feel better now."

"Alright. Why don't you wash yourself off and then go back to bed? You know where to find me if you get scared or need anything," she said as she walked out of the bathroom.

Bobby felt guilty about what he had done. But he felt better when he realized that his homework would be done for him now. He changed his pants, retrieved the twenty-dollar bill from the cabinet, put it in his schoolbag when he got to his room, and went to bed. The evening was a success.

When Bobby got up for school the following morning, his father had already left for work and his mother hurried him to get ready for the bus before she headed off to work, herself. There was no mention of what happened just a few hours earlier.

Bobby sat next to his friend Jeremy on the school bus.

"Hey, Bobby, catch the new episode of *Cathouse* on HBO? It's so cool. I saw boobies as big as my head, and I have a big head! My dad's cool and all for watching it while I'm in the room," Jeremy said.

"Nah, I must have missed it," Bobby said as if he were bored. He nonchalantly pulled out the twenty-dollar bill from his schoolbag and inspected it. "Doesn't Stonewall Jackson look cool on this bill?"

"Whoa, you got a whole twenty dollars? That's so cool!"

"I know. I just got my allowance. I didn't mow the lawn, so I only got half," Bobby said.

"Whoa! You must be rich!"

"We get by," Bobby responded arrogantly.

"Hey, wait a second. That's not that Stonewall Jackson on the twenty-dollar bill. That's Andrew Jackson. My uncle tested me on the presidents on dollar bills," Jeremy said.

"Doesn't really matter now, though, does it? That knowledge hasn't done anything for you. Who's the one with the dough?" Bobby replied.

"I suppose you're right. Say, you do those science review questions? I couldn't do them."

"Really? That's funny. I have it right here," Bobby said as he pulled out his notebook with the answers. "I found fifteen minutes to do them. It was a piece of cake."

"You're real smart, Bobby."

"What can I say?" Bobby said, forgetting he feigned pissing himself earlier that morning in order to pay his homework dealer.

The bus stopped in front of a house Bobby never noticed. A girl he had never seen before boarded. She wore zebra-striped pants, white sneakers, and a shirt that had an image of a rainbow stretched from shoulder to shoulder with an image of a unicorn on its hind legs underneath it. Its horn went through the rainbow, and a thought-bubble over the creature read, 'Dance Under the Rainbow.' Bobby was smitten. He made multiple glances at her throughout the bus ride. He didn't know how to approach her.

"Who's that girl?" He asked Jeremy and pointed to her.

"That girl? Who cares? Girls suck," Jeremy said. "It's boys all the way to the end. My dad says that will always be the case for me. He says that my boys will always be around, and that girls are skunks or something. He always says 'Bros before hoes.' He's been saying it ever since mom moved out of our house."

Bobby lost her in the crowd when they got to school. Her image was etched in his mind. He felt funny, and didn't know he was capable of feeling this way about someone. He realized that he needed tips from someone to learn how to contain these feelings; someone who's had a ton of experience with girls. He assumed that would be Charlie out of default. He felt his stomach fall to his feet when he saw her again at the front of his classroom. He couldn't believe his eyes.

"Class, this is Juliet. She just moved to the neighborhood, transferring here from where, Juliet?" Mrs. Harris asked.

"Trenton, New Jersey," Juliet said.

"Ah, yes, Trenton, which is the capital of New Jersey," Mrs. Harris said.

Bobby had never wanted to visit any place more than Trenton, New Jersey at that moment.

"You could have a seat at any open desk you'd like, Juliet, and welcome to our class!" Mrs. Harris said.

Bobby, oblivious of his surroundings, didn't realize the desk next to him was vacant. Juliet sat there, making him so nervous that he thought he'd piss his pants for real this time.

"So, Juliet, tomorrow is Mentor Day. Your classmates will bring a mentor of theirs to class, and then they will talk to us about what it means to be a role model. They will also submit a report about the person they chose. Since you're new to our class, you're exempt from this project. I trust that everyone else has someone in mind?" Mrs. Harris asked the class.

Bobby had forgotten about this assignment. He couldn't get his father because he was always too busy. He knew the right person he had to ask to fill the role. He also knew it was going to be a painstaking task to convince Charlie to come to his class – and write a paper on himself. The feeling of urination shifted to a feeling of nausea. Bobby thought the best thing to do to make himself feel better was to impress Juliet. He reached into his schoolbag and took out the twenty-dollar bill. He stared at it and flicked it with his middle finger. He knew the sound was annoying enough to make her look at him. She did, and accidentally made eye contact while doing so.

"I just got my allowance this morning. It's only half," Bobby said as he pointed at the bill and shrugged his shoulders.

Juliet had a blank expression. Bobby kept quiet for the rest of class and didn't want to try anything until he got advice from Charlie.

Bobby rang Charlie's doorbell later that afternoon.

"B-man, good to see you. You get that twenty dollars? I need it pronto," Charlie said as he opened the door.

"Yeah, here it is," Bobby said and handed it over to him.

"Alright, come on in, then."

"Will you finish the rest of the homework for me now?"

"Yeah, already got it finished. I did it yesterday so you wouldn't have to bother me about it today. Did you pretend to piss yourself?"

"Yeah, I did. I splashed toilet water on my pants and went in there."

"Whoa, that's hoss, dude. You're definitely the man of the day. That took some ingenuity. For that, you get a Klondike bar. There's half of one I didn't finish earlier today. Knock yourself out, dude, you've earned it."

"I need you to do me another favor."

"Another solid? Oh, man, you're cramping my style, B-man."

"I need you to come to my class tomorrow. You need do this mentor thing. I also need you to write a one-page essay about why you're my mentor."

"Fuck that and fuck you, my little man. No way, no how."

"Aww, come on Charlie! I need you to do this for me! I can't find anyone else!"

"B-man, I'll feel like a weirdo going to your school. What am I gonna say, 'Hey, Bobby's the kid who I hang out with. We watch karate movies together, eat ice cream bars, and watch dog fights.' They'll have the authorities on me in minutes. I'm not going to have my face posted on every streetlamp again; not this time, not this neighborhood!"

"What are you talking about?"

"Nothing, B-man, nothing. Sorry, can't do it."

"Please? I'll do anything!"

"Anything? You do realize this is going to be way more than twenty dollars-worth of stuff, right?"

"Yeah, I know. It's just that I also want to impress this new girl in class. If she sees that I'm friends with you, she'll think I'm cool, and that I hang out with older guys who ride mountain bikes."

"Whoa, tell me about this girl, B-man. What's she like? What's she packing?"

"Well, she's in my class. She's about my height, and she likes unicorns."

"She's into unicorns? Piece of cake. You're in like Flynn, little dude."

"What should I do to make her like me?"

"Well, for starters, don't be a dweeb next to her or make it seem as if you asked me for advice. She needs to know that you're naturally a cool dude, you know? You should seem like you're not interested. Be sort of a dick to her without *really* being a dick, ya' know?"

"No, I don't follow."

"Like, ignore her at times, but don't like hit her. Only six year old boys are into hitting girls – and besides, they're used merchandise. You're into eight year olds. That's prime time for you, man."

"Yeah, prime time."

"Ask her out to the movies. Go see some cheesy shit like *When Harry Met Sally* – or in your case, some bullshit about superhero dogs or something."

"Really? And then what?"

"Well, while you're at the movies, be like, 'We gonna make out or what? I got shit to do, lady....' Girls melt over that sort of thing. It makes you look like you've got things to do. You manipulate her like silly putty."

"What is make out?"

"That's when you shove your tongue into a girl's mouth and lick her tongue."

"Eww, that's gross."

"You let your dog lick you in the face, right?"

"Yeah."

"Same thing."

"What if she doesn't want to make out with me?"

"Punch her in the muff."

"Huh?"

"Nothing, I was joking. Don't worry about it, she'll make out with you."

"How long do we make out for?"

"Until the b.j."

"B.J.'s? Why would we go to B.J.'s? My parents are members. They buy huge toilet paper rolls there. Why does she need *that much* toilet paper?"

"Trust me, everyone likes to go to B.J.'s. Maybe you shouldn't be doing that right now at your age. Just stick with making out. That's like going all the way in the kid world. You tell me you made out with the girl, you're the man and no one's got shit on you. This girl's in your class? I'll see her tomorrow if I go?"

"Yeah! Please come, it'll be so much fun!"

"Alright, I'll go, but you owe me big time. First off, you just reminded me that I need to wash my mountain bike. You're going to clean it for me. And you owe me another thing that will come at a future date."

"Deal!"

"You hustle me, we've got problems, B-man. I know where you live and what your mother looks like. Remember when I ran into you guys at the supermarket that one time? I never forget a face."

"Yes, I promise I'm not lying to you. Will you also write the one-page essay?"

"Fine. While I write it up, you could watch the DVD I got today that has freak deaths caught on tape. One of them has surveillance footage of this old lady who tripped while crossing train tracks and got her head crushed by a freight train. It's totally funny!"

"Yeah, put that in for me!"

"You got it, dude…"

Charlie started working on the paper about himself. He made himself seem to be a standup citizen. He wrote about the time he adopted a baby and donated it to charity; about the time he donated a kidney to the diabetic with an amputated foot; and about how he worked at an after-school big brother program where he tutored and played basketball with children like Bobby.

The next day was Mentor Day. Bobby's parents were unaware such a day existed at his school.

Jeremy brought in his father's A.A. sponsor; Alicia Keschler brought in her grandmother; Vinny Grimaldi brought in his father Vinny, Sr.; Bobby brought in Charlie, marathon runner, kidney donor, charity giver, parent of an adopted child, and mentor. On paper, he was a hero to every child in America.

Each student spoke of harrowing tales of virtue in their mentor's introduction. Mentors spoke for about five minutes. Alicia Keschler's grandmother baked cupcakes for everyone.

When it was Bobby's turn, he stood in front of the class next to Charlie and introduced him by saying, "Everything I learned about being a man I learned from Charlie Ferrigno." Everyone clapped for

Charlie.

"Thank you, Bobby, for that cool intro. Hey, dudes, what's up? You have a pretty cool school here. You guys have a ton of chips in your vending machines. When I was a kid, we didn't have as many options. We had Daisy Doodles, which Fritos kind of ripped off. What's up with that? So, anyway, I wanted to be a firefighter, but I failed a drug test. I then did all the stuff in Bobby's bio on me – the kidney stuff, marathons, adoptions. After doing all that, I ended up working at Taco Bill's. You know that place? Yeah, I work there from time to time to make ends meet. I also run an after-school program where I tutor and hang out with dweebs like Bobby. Hey, Bobby, just kidding, fuggedaboutit!"

"Hey!" Vinny Grimaldi, Sr. said in approval.

"So, yeah, I rock out a lot of times. I go to concerts and donated a kidney, but I already mentioned that part. I also have an extensive collection of totally awesome stuff on DVD. If you kids ever wanna come by, just ask Bobby where I live. Alright, I don't have anything else to say to you. This sucked more than grandma over there. At least she brought in cupcakes, right? Just kidding, ma'am. Thanks, dudes, and if you're ever gonna get into music when you get older, I recommend Bruce Springsteen's *Born in the U.S.A.* be your first album. It was mine, and I still listen to it at Taco Bill's. Rock on, dudes. Hey, Bobby, which is the girl you like?" Charlie said.

Everyone in the room started laughing, and boys made catcalls at Bobby. Charlie tried to cover his tracks.

"Just kidding! Gotcha, you little perverts," Charlie said to the class and sat down.

The mentors were allowed to eat with the students in the cafeteria at lunchtime. Charlie constantly complained about the food.

"This is supposed to be a fucking hamburger?" He said.

"Yes, now please keep it down, Charlie. These are my classmates," Bobby said.

"How the fuck could you eat this shit? This is some sort of child abuse. Fuck this, I ain't eating it. Hey, was the girl you liked in the classroom?"

"Yeah, she was."

"Which one was she?"

"She sits right next to me."

"Oh, yeah? B-man, did I just up your game in there or what?"

"I don't know what you mean."

"Did I improve your chances with her? You don't have to answer that because I know I did. You're going to have her eating out of your hand. You know what you have to do now, right? Close your hand and trap her beak. Get it?"

"No, not really."

"Hey, wanna see something cool? Where's your bathroom?" Charlie said without explaining what he meant by his beak metaphor.

"Follow me," Bobby said as he led Charlie to the boys' restroom.

Charlie started laughing like a giddy schoolboy when they went inside.

"Ugh, it stinks in here," Charlie said.

"What does it stink like?" Bobby asked.

"What you'd think it stinks like…shit, you fucking doof."

"Oh, yeah."

"Doesn't matter because this is going to be so classic," Charlie said.

Charlie went into a stall and locked himself in. He then got on his hands and knees, and crawled into the other stall. He locked that stall, too, and crawled out from underneath the door. His palms were covered in hair, grime, and piss stains.

"It's kind of gross, but it was totally worth it. The kids are gonna flip when they see that the stalls are locked and no one's inside. This is gonna cause mass chaos in the school. The administrators are gonna flip a fucking lid, and you're gonna witness it. Well, gotta jet, B-man. I've got things to do. Remember about the girl. Ask her if she wants to ride bikes or something one day after school. Girls always wanna ride bikes. It's their kryptonite."

"Really? That will make me like Flynn?"

"The fuck are you talking about?"

"You said yesterday that I would be in like your friend Flynn."

"Yeah, dude, in like Flynn. You're totally gonna get the digits, or in your case a screen name at least, and you could chat with her past your bedtime. That's how I met my internet girlfriends, and not one of them has cheated on me. I can't say the same about myself. I'm like a caged tiger that sneaks out every so often while the zookeeper's asleep, you know what I mean? I have like four internet girlfriends I'm cheating on right now."

"I don't understand, Charlie."

"You will when you get older, you will. Anyway, gotta jet, B-man. I'll talk to you later."

"Alright, Charlie, thanks for coming. Maybe you should wash your hands. They're gross."

"Based on the poor quality of the burgers in the cafeteria, I wouldn't trust their soap, so don't think so. I'll talk to you later, B-man," Charlie said as he rubbed Bobby's head with his grimy hands. For the record, no one ever made a fuss about the stalls being locked. They were simply unlocked again after lunchtime.

Charlie decided to walk to the park to spy on mothers watching their children play at the playground. On the way, he stopped by a deli to get a sandwich and saw the butcher he had a crush on. Her name was Janice. Her father owned the place. She'd usually give Charlie extra cheese on his sandwich.

"Hey, Janice, how's it going?" Charlie asked.

"Hi, Charlie, it's a pleasant surprise to see you here at this time."

"Yeah, I had to give this talk at a school."

"Really? What for?"

"I'm a part of the community thing where I talk to kids about the dangers of drugs and persuade them from doing that, touching cigarettes, or smelling alcohol from their stepfathers' breaths. You know, the usual," Charlie said, completely making it up.

"That's so nice. I love children. I think it's really cool that you're into that. It's hard to find someone who devotes time to them."

"Someone's gotta do it. Who's it gonna be, your dad?" Charlie said, but immediately realized that wasn't a good idea because he remembered Janice's father had suffered four heart attacks and was practically on his last leg. He tried to recover, "...because he has to stay here and watch the deli."

"Yeah, this place is his baby," Janice said and laughed.

"Yeah, wah, wah..." Charlie said. He then spilled water onto the floor from an open bottle on the counter by the register, "Oops, looks like someone wet his diaper. Goo-goo-ga-ga."

"You're a funny guy, Charlie."

"Hey-oooooo!"

"Stop it, stop it, you're slaying me."

"Once you wind me up, there's no stop button."

"What are you doing later today?"

"Me? I have nothing to do. I'm free. Totally free. Why? Wanna hang out?" Charlie said as blunt and honestly as possible.

"Yes, I'd love to. I get out of here around seven. Why don't you come over then and we could get some dinner? I'm sick of sandwiches and Fritos. How does that sound?"

"I say it sounds like stupendous idea, Miss Janice. I shall be here promptly at seven to escort you to a most wonderful restaurant. Alright, well, I'll see you then," Charlie said and walked out of the deli. He returned five minutes later. "I forgot to order my sandwich. Could I have a turkey with American cheese, lettuce, tomato, mayo, salt, pepper, and vinegar? Hold the fur!"

"Of course you can, Charlie."

He was afraid to break her concentration and blow it, so he was quiet as she made him the sandwich.

"We're still on for tonight, right?" He asked when she handed the sandwich to him.

"Of course, why wouldn't we be?"

"Nah, just checking. Cool. I'll see you then. I'll go pay your father for this now. I'll see you tonight."

Charlie paid Janice's father and yelled out, "Seven o'clock, be here," and left, thinking he made a cool exit.

Charlie believed he was the funniest and most charming man in town. He wanted Bobby to help him get ready for his date, but saw it was only one-thirty. He went to the nearest drug store to buy a pack of condoms, but couldn't decide which to purchase.

"So many fucking options of this shit these days," he said to himself as he examined the labels for each pack. He read through an assortment of condom types, including ribbed, lambskin, ultra-thin, flavored.

"Ribbed for *her* pleasure? What about for *my* pleasure?" He said. An elderly woman walking past him gave him a dirty look. Forty-five minutes later, he chose the glow-in-the-dark ones. He left the boxes he was analyzing disorganized on a shelf.

"How bright does this get?" He asked the cashier, referring to the glow-in-the-dark condoms.

"I don't know what you mean, sir," the cashier responded.

"Like, will I be able to use my dick as a flashlight in the dark? Does it get that bright?"

The cashier laughed. Charlie didn't laugh along with him.

"What's so funny? It's a serious question. Can I use it as a flashlight in the dark?"

"I doubt it."

"Then what's the point of it?"

"I don't know. Fun? I think it would be used for fun?"

"I'm talking to genius of the year. Condoms are used for fun. Can I quote you on that, Jason?" Charlie said, reading the cashier's nametag.

"Yeah, I think you can, but please don't use the name of the store. It's against policy."

Charlie made his way to Bobby's school after leaving the drug store, hoping to intercept him. He had a bandana and sunglasses on as he stood outside the school waiting for Bobby to be dismissed. Class after class walked out through the school gate. Charlie eventually caught a glimpse of Bobby, and grabbed him by the arm.

"You're coming with me," Charlie said.

"Huh?" Bobby said, startled. "Oh, Charlie! You scared me!"

"Shut up and let's go. We only have four hours."

"Where are we going? Four hours?"

They walked across the street and waited at the bus stop.

"I have a date tonight. I told you that you needed to act cool to be cool. I'm the living example," Charlie said.

"Really? With who?"

"This babe from the deli. She just threw herself at me after my awesome charisma hypnotized her. These eyes are an aphrodisiac. That's why I have to wear sunglasses."

"You're talking funny, Charlie," Bobby said and laughed.

"Shut up, loser. I don't see you with any dates tonight. I don't hear you talking about that bitch you like. I bet you didn't even talk to her. Am I right?"

"No, but—"

"I knew it. Look at me. I grabbed the bull by the horns and let it blow me, and now I'm surfing a tidal wave of awesome."

"But you told me to ignore her and make it seem as if I'm not interested!"

"No, I didn't."

"Oh. I must have heard you wrong then."

"Obviously."

"Why are we waiting here at the bus stop?"

"To catch a fucking submarine. We're waiting here to catch the bus, genius. What's with you today?"

"But, where are we going?"

"We're going to Macy's."

"Are you going to buy your date something nice?"

"Fuck that—" Charlie said with an angry look on his face.

"What happened? Are you alright?"

"Yeah, I was going to fart as a response to you asking if I was going to buy her something, but it didn't come out. You asked, 'Are you going to buy her something nice?' and I was going to say, 'Fuck that,' and then fart pretty loudly. It would have been hilarious. And being funny and charming is what got me this date, so learn from me. Here comes the bus. You have a bus pass or something?"

"Yeah."

"Do you have a dollar?"

"I think I do. I didn't buy any chips today."

"Hand it over, then. I only have enough for one way."

Bobby handed his dollar to Charlie as the bus stopped next to them. They boarded it and headed to Macy's. They went straight to the perfume section when they got there. Charlie got free samples of cologne sprayed on him. He took scent cards and rubbed them all over his body for forty-five minutes.

"Alright, we're done here. Bobby, you should rub these cards on yourself and not take a shower tonight or tomorrow morning. That way, you'll smell like a rock star after his awesome sold out gig at Madison Square Garden," Charlie said as he sprayed Bobby with cologne while rubbing his chest with the scent cards. "When your mother asks you why you smell like cologne, tell her you and some kid were goofing off."

After they took the bus back into town, Charlie walked Bobby home as close as he could without going out of his way.

"Alright, B-man, the deli is four blocks from here. You walk the rest home. I'll talk to you later," Charlie said. "Remember, you've got the power now that you smell like a million bucks. Use it to talk to that girl you like. It's time to make power moves."

"Goodnight, Charlie, and thanks for the advice. I'll try to talk to her tomorrow. Good luck! I hope you and your date go to B.J.'s together."

Charlie casually walked to the deli, but his heart was pounding. He couldn't remember the last time he was as nervous as he was at that moment. When he arrived, he saw Janice restocking canned soups on a shelf with her back turned to the front entrance. He took off his sunglasses and bandana, and slowly crept towards her.

"You have the right to remain sexy, baby!" He said.

Janice shrieked and fell to the floor.

"Shit! Charlie! Don't you ever do that to me again. I almost smashed your head in with this can," Janice said. "Seriously, I hate it when people creep up behind me. Now, help me up."

"Sorry. I get carried away sometimes. Remember, I'm like a winding doll that has no stop button."

"Whatever. You have like sixteen pounds of cologne on, ugh. What did you put on?"

"Oh, just a little bit of this, a little bit of that. It's not a big deal, really. Most of it is natural scent," he said thinking what she said was a compliment. "So, you wanna head outta here? What are you in the mood for?"

"How about some Chinese?" Janice recommended.

"No way, I hate that Chinese shit. How about some nice Mexican?"

"Sure, that sounds alright. What do you have in mind?"

"I know where we could get hooked up pretty well."

He ended up taking her to where he works, Taco Bill's. He had the cook Enrique make tacos and burritos.

"I told you we'd get hooked up. Enrique is taking a third of the full price off of the check. Where else would you find that?" Charlie said.

"Nowhere, I suppose," Janice said with a disappointed look on her face.

"Why the long face?" He asked.

"I was just kind of hoping we could go to a nice restaurant, not some fast food place."

"Nah, this is cool. We're getting the royal treatment. Look where we're sitting, right next to the kitchen. No one gets to sit here!"

"Probably because it's so hot back here."

"Nah, you're crazy. It's exclusive."

"Excuse me," a patron said, requesting Charlie move the chair he was sitting in forward so he could walk into the restroom, which was located next to their table.

"Oh, sure," Charlie said and slid his chair forward to let the man pass. "Yeah, it's a little annoying when people have to ask us to move because they can't get into the bathroom, but I bet you that while that guy's taking a piss at the urinal right now, he's thinking to himself, 'Wow, that couple is pretty fucking cool. Everyone at the restaurant knows who they are.'"

"Yes, I'm sure he is thinking just that, Charlie."

"That's weird. I seem to have forgotten my wallet on my toilet seat this afternoon," Charlie said thinking fast on his feet.

"It's alright, I've got it covered."

Janice didn't look like she had a good time at Taco Bill's, so Charlie thought he'd take her to the arcade.

"Wanna to go to the arcade down at the mall?" He asked.

"Sure, that sounds like fun," she responded.

"I don't have a car at the moment. The insurance company is on my ass, so I can't legally—"

"It's alright, I'll drive," Janice said.

At the arcade, they played foosball, air hockey, and went outdoors to play mini-golf. Janice paid for everything. She didn't mind because she was beginning to have a good time with Charlie. When she drove him home later that evening, he asked if she wanted to come in for a nightcap.

"Wanna get crunked?" He asked.

"Do you mean a drink?" She asked.

"Yeah, sloshed, wasted, fucked up, bonked, whatever terminology you use. I have beers in my fridge. Wanna come in? It'll be fun. I have a DVD collection that suits every interest. You work at a deli, so you might like the new one I got. It's surveillance footage of freak accidents at Vietnamese slaughterhouses. It's hysterical!"

"As tempting as that sounds, I think I'll have to pass on watching the DVD. But, how about we go to my place instead?"

"Shit, that's an even better idea," he said as he started grooming himself in front of the side mirror. "Looks like these aren't gonna be a waste after all." He pulled out the pack of glow-in-the-dark condoms and threw it onto the dashboard.

"What's that?" She asked. "Are those condoms?"

"Yeah, they were starting to be a drag in my pocket. We *are* going to have sex tonight, right?"

Janice gave him a puzzled look. She took the pack and put it in her purse.

She had second thoughts about stepping inside Charlie's house and experiencing what he was into, first-hand, considering she had already experienced enough already. She thought there was something alluring about him, though, and appreciated his confidence in buying a pack of condoms for a first date. When they got to her apartment, he was impressed with how big it was considering she worked at a deli.

"How could you afford this?" Charlie asked.

"Working my ass off."

"Working at the deli gets you this? You're barely even there! I really need to reconsider my life."

"Well, I get paid off the books, and my father's the owner."

"Damn, could I work there?"

"Are you serious? Because if you are, I could see what I could do. You'd be making a lot more than you do at Taco Bill's, I could tell you that for sure."

"How do you know I don't make a ton at Taco Bill's?"

"Charlie, we're talking about Taco Fucking Bill's."

"Yeah, you're right. It'd be really cool if you could get me a job at the deli."

"Want a beer?" Janice said as she pulled out two Bud Lights from her refrigerator.

"Yeah, gimme one."

They drank, talked, and watched television on her futon. She then started talking about her favorite movie, *When Harry Met Sally*.

"You've never seen that movie? It's to die for! I love Billy Crystal," Janice said.

"Nope, sorry, never have."

"You have to watch it!" She said as she took it out to play on her DVD player. Charlie turned the lights off.

He was bored ten minutes into it. He drank more to make the movie enjoyable for himself. By the forty-five-minute mark, he was so drunk that he couldn't sit up anymore. It was at the forty-six-minute mark when Janice started kissing him. It was at the fifty-minute mark when both of their clothes were off. It was at the fifty-two-minute mark when Janice pulled out the condom pack, took a glow-in-the-dark condom out, and put it on Charlie. It was at the fifty-four-minute mark when they were finished and shut the movie off.

They had sex again forty-five minutes later. Later that night, Charlie got up to get another beer from the refrigerator.

"Look at my glow-in-the-dark dick swing from side-to-side as I walk," he said and laughed.

"So, Charlie, how'd you like the movie?" Janice asked.

"The movie sucked. I liked when you blew me better," he said as he took a sip out of a Bud Light bottle.

"You're all about blowjobs and Buds, aren't you?"

"That's right. I'm a pretty cool guy," he said as he began to chug the beer. "I'm up for round three," he continued after he drank all the beer in the bottle and belched.

"Oh, are you?"

"Yeah, got the condom on already. So, spread those lips, I'm cummin' in."

"Wait, I don't remember you ever putting on another condom before we did it the second time. Did you use the same condom twice? You didn't take it off after the first time?" Janice asked.

"Oh, yeah, that's gross," Charlie said, and then rolled the condom off his penis and threw it onto the carpet.

"What are you doing? Don't throw that on the floor! The semen will seep into the carpet, you idiot," Janice said.

"Sorry, where's your garbage anyway?"

"You're standing next to the trash can, genius."

"Oh, that's right. You have any gloves or something so I could pick it up?"

"Just pick it up with your hands!"

"But that's gross…"

"It's *your* semen!"

"So? I don't put my fingers into my piss stream, you know?"

"You fucked me twice using the same condom without ever taking it off, so it's already beyond gross."

"Alright, fine. I'll pick it up with my fingers and throw it out. This is so gross," he said as he picked up the condom and threw it into the garbage bin. "You know this shit smells, too, right?"

"Shut up. Come back to the futon and let's go to sleep. I have to be at work at seven in the morning, but doubt that's happening."

"Scoot over, I don't want half of my body off of it," Charlie said.

Janice woke up at eleven forty-five in the morning to find Charlie staring at her lying in bed.

"Charlie! You scared the shit out of me."

"You look so peaceful when you're asleep," he responded.

"You stared at me while I slept? For how long?"

"Not long. Like two and a half hours."

"Don-don-don't you ever do that again."

"Alright....don't know what the big deal is, but alright..."

"Anyway, I have to get ready for work and go. You could stay if you'd like."

"Nah, I'm gonna jet, too."

"Ok. So, what are you doing tonight?"

"Nothing. Why? Do you wanna hang out with me again?" He said incredulously.

"Yeah, I do. I had fun with you last night."

"Oh, wow, really? Shit, well in that case, I'm always around. Gimme a call."

"No, I'd prefer you stopped by the deli again when I close up."

"Sure, I could do that."

"Shouldn't you be going to work, yourself?"

"Don't really feel like it today. It's cool, though. I've only gotten one notice about backed rent."

"Oh. I'll get back to you about the deli job. I'm going to step into the shower. I'll see you tonight. Lock up when you leave," she said as she closed the bathroom door.

Charlie was surprised everything worked out for him. He was excited that a real girl was interested in him. The sex with Janice was the best sex he had since the party he threw his first week in college that got him expelled.

He went straight home, bypassing the playground with the hot moms, and watched some of his pornographic DVD's to examine various sexual positions in them. He thought he'd impress Janice if he were a sexual dynamo. Bobby knocked on his door a few hours later.

"B-man, what's up, dude?" Charlie answered.

"Something terrible happened," Bobby said.

"Really? Could have fooled me. It's been a pretty good day for me."

"Juliet doesn't like me. I think I scared her during recess."

"How'd you blow it? By the way, I love the way you smell. The combination of last night's cologne mixed with your sweat makes a pungent, yet satisfying scent."

"Thanks. The tips you gave me didn't work."

"What? That's impossible. Come in and tell me what happened."

"Well, I saw her sitting alone during recess tying her shoes. I sat down next to her and said, 'Hey, Juliet, wanna ride bikes sometime with me? I have this nifty Huffy that has a few gears. I like to ride fast.' At first, she seemed like she was interested. She seemed excited. Then I said, 'So, you wanna make out or what? I got shit to do, lady...' She didn't like that I cussed, and said I had a dirty mouth. She also said she's not the kind of girl who makes out. She said she saw her mother and father do it once, and they told her that it's a way that boys hurt girls, and that she shouldn't do that with a boy until she was twenty-one years old because it won't hurt as much. She then told me that she doesn't want to ride bikes with me anymore. Making out hurts girls. Why did you want me to hurt her, Charlie? I like her, I don't want to hurt her!"

"You got lied to, Bobby. Girls play that trick a lot. Trust me. Girls like to lie. It's what they're good at. They can't fight or play sports, so they lie."

"Why would she lie about that? What did I do to her? Why won't she like me back?"

"You got fucked, B-man. You learned a vital lesson today. Life has struck again and kicked you in the nuts. It's what I taught you the other day. Remember? But, don't fret. There are a ton of other warthogs in the barn."

"How did your date go?"

"Mine went awesomely. I like her a lot."

"Is she also a warthog?"

"I will slap you across the mouth if you say that about her again. She's a nice girl."

"Sorry, Charlie."

"Apology not accepted at this time. Anyway, she's a good girl, and I have another date with her tonight."

"So, is she your girlfriend?"

"Yeah."

"Are you two getting married?"

"Most likely."

"Are you two in love?"

"Very."

"That's good news! Say, could you do my science homework for me?"

"Sorry, B-man, I can't today. I need to head down to the deli soon."

"But it's a midterm review!"

"Listen, Bobby, I'm not gonna be there to take the midterm with you. You're gonna have to learn this shit for yourself. What the fuck are you gonna do when you're my age and not know fundamental shit, like the difference between a plant and animal cell? You know how many times that shit's popped up and paid off after you're done with school? Like a million! I'd start cracking on the books if I were you."

"But Charlie, I can't start reading stuff from the beginning of the trimester! Look at how many chapters it covers!"

"Yeah, three chapters, each about ten pages long. It's nothing, B-man. Anyway, I can't do it. I need to time to get my awesome on for tonight."

"Fine, Charlie, just go ahead and ruin my life! Goodbye!" Bobby said as he slammed the door and ran home.

Charlie brushed off Bobby's fit and continued to get ready for his date. He picked up Janice at the deli that evening. They went to the movie theater to see the latest Hugh Grant movie. Janice was a big fan of his. She loved his accent. Charlie spent the night at her apartment once again. He began to spend nights there frequently.

Within the next month, Charlie quit his job at Taco Bill's and started working at Janice's father's deli full-time. He started spending less and less time with Bobby. Charlie made his new girlfriend a priority, and didn't have time for anything or anyone else. Meanwhile, Bobby's grades took a nosedive at school, causing his parents to raise concern.

"Bobby, you got a D on the science midterm? Don't you pay attention in class?" His mother asked.

"I try to, but I can't understand it, mom. It's too hard for me!"

"This isn't good. John, could you look over and check Bobby's homework each night?" Bobby's mother asked his father.

"Liz, you know that when I get home, I just want to relax and have some alone time. I get hassled enough at work. Bobby, try harder or we're getting you a tutor," his father said. "Why don't *you* check his homework, Liz?"

"I barely have any time to make dinner. It looks like we're going to have to find you a tutor, Bobby. John, will you remind yourself tomorrow at work to at least find one for him?"

"Fine, Liz, and while I'm at it, why don't I stop by Mr. Robertson's office and tell him to go fuck himself, too?"

"John! You *will* watch your mouth when Bobby is in the room! What's wrong with you? Bobby, go to your room and play with your toys. I think Duke is in there waiting for you," Bobby's mother said.

Bobby went to his room, listening to his parents argue as he walked upstairs. He remembered his father forgot to complain about Mrs. Harris, which was good news for him. He decided to do his homework for once. He began reading his textbooks, which was something he never would have done if he weren't left high and dry by Charlie. As much as he was disappointed in Charlie, Bobby missed his company. It had been weeks since they saw each other. Each time Bobby made an effort to see him, Charlie would say he was busy.

Bobby went to Charlie's house one day unannounced. Janice answered the door.

"Hi, is Charlie home?"

"Who are you?" Janice asked him.

"I'm Bobby. I'm a friend of Charlie's."

"A friend of his? I've never seen you before."

"We used to hang out like every day. Is he here?"

"One second," she said and screamed out Charlie's name, never taking her eyes off of Bobby. Charlie came to the door, shirtless.

"Oh, hey, B-man, what's up? Janice, could I have some time alone with him?"

"Uh, sure," Janice said in a confused tone and left them alone.

"Charlie, could I watch some more DVD's today?" Bobby asked.

"What are you doing here?" Charlie asked.

"I'm here to hang out. Is that your girlfriend?"

"Yeah. Hey, B-man, it's a little weird for you to be here. Janice already thinks I'm a weirdo, so I don't need her to know that I hang out with little kids."

"But, it's been a while since I watched some DVD's at your house. I'm sure you got new ones."

"I stopped subscribing to that sort of stuff. Janice doesn't like it."

"Why doesn't she like it? Those dog fights and freak accidents were so funny!"

"I know, right? I don't know, man. I think it was time I grew up, you know? I'm thirty-six years old. I don't really do the kid stuff anymore. I don't even work at Taco Bill's anymore. I'm moving up. I work at the deli now."

"Wow, really?"

"It's the truth, little dude. I'm gonna be trained on the electric cutter next week."

"That's big news, Charlie."

"I know. It's upscale shit. Anyway, I should get going. Janice and I are going out for dinner."

"Where are you going?"

"We're going to some sushi place."

"Eww, I thought you hated sushi."

"Yeah, I do, but she likes it, you know?"

"Are you happy, Charlie? You look sad, and you're not as fun anymore."

"It's all a part of growing up, you know? I have to adapt to it. You'll understand when you're older. It's just that whenever you meet a girl who's a lot hotter than you are, you have to adapt. I couldn't care less what goes on in my life, or that any fun is sapped right out of it, just as long as I get laid regularly and have a pretty hot girlfriend. Again, you'll realize this when you get older."

"Wow, Charlie," Bobby said.

"Yeah, I know."

Janice came back to the door.

"So, Charlie, you ready for dinner? Are you done here with the kid?"

"Uh, gimme a second, Janice, I'm still talking to him."

"Well, hurry up. I'm hungry," she said and walked back inside.

Charlie rolled his eyes and whispered, "She's so much hotter than I am, so you know…"

"Yeah, I know," Bobby responded.

"So, any updates on that girl you liked?"

"No, we don't really speak. I don't even sit next to her anymore. Mrs. Harris put me in the front of the classroom because I started falling behind in my grades."

"Sorry, B-man. I hope you're actually starting to study."

"Yeah, I'm reading from the textbook. I guess you taught me a good lesson. I really do need to learn this stuff on my own. I may be getting a tutor."

"Really?"

"Yeah, my parents want to get me one."

"That sucks, man, tutors could be huge buzzkills. Hey, come in for a second. I gotta take a shit."

"But won't your girlfriend be mad?"

"She'll get over it. Trust me, I've done worse."

Bobby stepped into the house and stood in the living room. Janice walked into the living room when she heard Charlie go into the bathroom.

"What are you still doing here?" She asked.

"Charlie asked me to come in. Why are you being so bossy and mean to me?"

"Listen, kid, I don't know who you are, but you learn to respect your elders. Don't talk back to me. I hate kids, and you look just as annoying as any other."

"I didn't do anything to you!"

"How do you know Charlie? The next thing I need is to find out that either he's molesting you or that you're his kid that he's been hiding from me."

"I don't know, we're just friends. He used to do my homework and we'd watch movies together. We like a lot of the same things."

"That's pretty weird."

"I don't know."

"Listen, you're interrupting our evening, why don't you get out of here?"

"But, I'm waiting for Charlie. He's my friend. He's my best friend."

"Why don't you find friends your own age? Your awkward face annoys me."

"What's wrong with my face?"

"You just look like a weird kid. Get lost. You're not welcome here anymore. Charlie doesn't even like you. If he did, then he'd have mentioned you or you'd be around more often."

"That's not true. Take it back."

"Looks like your best friend doesn't like you. Just get out of here."

"Shut up," Bobby said and started to cry.

"Oh, are you going to start crying? Get out of here. Leave now. I'm tired of this shit," Janice said as she grabbed Bobby by the collar and dragged him out of the living room, through the front door. He cried louder and ran home. Charlie heard the commotion while sitting on the toilet. He came out of the bathroom without wiping.

"What the fuck is going on out here?" He asked.

"I dragged that fucking annoying kid out of here. What's your relation to him anyway? Is he your kid or something? Don't you lie to me..."

"No, why would you think that? That's fucking horrible. What's your beef with him? He's a good kid."

"I hate kids. I never liked kids, and I was depressed I was one during the years I was one. They're fucking brats. I would never want to have kids. I can't imagine how a mother could live with a baby or a kid and not want to bash its brains in."

"I thought you liked kids. When we went on our first date, you were impressed that I spoke to them about staying away from drugs — which was actually bullshit, but you didn't know that then."

"What, and make myself seem like a bitch if I said I didn't like kids the day we went on our first date? Besides, I knew you were a loser, and I knew that story was bullshit. You're a weird enough guy as it is, Charlie, why hang out with that kid?"

"Knew I was a loser? What are you talking about?"

"As if I have to draw you a fucking picture? Just look around. Look at this place. Your life was shit before you met me."

"We've only been dating for a couple of months."

"And what a couple of months it's been for you. You're growing up, finally, at thirty-six years old. You're much better off. You only looked cool and like a superhero to a fucking kid before you met me. Grow the fuck up. Maybe that's why you acted so childish, because you hung out with him."

"I can't believe you don't like kids," Charlie said. "I love kids."

"Apparently, weirdo," Janice said.

"I don't like this at all. How could stand yourself after making him cry?"

"He'll get over it, Charlie. I doubt it'll haunt him into his teenage years. He'll be even more of an annoying fuck when he reaches that stage of his life."

Charlie ruminated to himself. He was unhappy and disappointed in himself for changing who he was for someone. He was content in doing what he wanted to, whenever he wanted to. He didn't want to be miserable like Bobby's parents. Bobby would often complain about them to him, and Charlie told himself he'd make sure his life never turned out as bland as theirs. He wanted to pursue his own happiness, on his terms. He thought it was admirable to be looked upon as a superhero by children. Janice, on the other hand, thought he was a joke before they started dating. Charlie wasn't going to surrender his virtues anymore.

"You know, get the fuck out. Any asshole who makes a kid cry like that and kicks him out without him doing anything wrong just speaks volumes about what a dick you are. I'm a pretty fucking cool guy. I like blowjobs and Buds, yeah, but I'm still going to be unhappy each time after I blow a load when I'm with you. You're a reminder to me that I'm turning into a sucker and square. I like doing the things I like to do, and I have pretty cool friends who are into pretty cool stuff. It doesn't matter how old they are. If you could shit the shit, you're in good shape."

"What?"

"Lemme say it in a way you'll understand – get the fuck out. I quit your daddy's job, and I never wanna see you again. I guess I was born a loser and I'll always be a loser. One thing's for sure, though. At least I'll be fucking happy."

"Fuck you!"

"No, fuck you and your shitty ass fucking movies! I hated *When Harry Met Sally*. I hated it so much!"

"It's because you've got zero class! You probably didn't understand the jokes, Neanderthal!" Janice said as she stormed out of the house.

Charlie didn't know what to do now that Janice was out of his life. The only thing to do in that instance when you don't know what to do is to drink until you pass out, and that's exactly what he did.

He woke up the next morning with a hangover and a worried feeling. He didn't know how he'd be able to pay his rent now that he lost his job at the deli. He remembered a job proposition his former drug dealer once made to him – a scientific study where he'd have to perform oral pleasure to men with a variety of ailments to see how it impacts their sexual desires.

"Looks like I'm gonna have to suck dick for science," he told himself. He stood in his living room and thought a while longer to truly see if he had no further options. He suddenly had an epiphany.

That afternoon, he ran to Bobby's school to see Mrs. Harris. She remembered him as Bobby's mentor. He gave her a flyer he made on loose-leaf paper with his phone number and information about Charlie Ferrigno's After-School Center, an after-school tutoring program run from his home. When asked about any accreditation, Charlie assured he was accredited, and so no further information was needed. He got the best of everyone with his catlike improvisational skills.

A few months later, Charlie's apartment became an after-school tutoring haven for kids at the local elementary school. Everyone in Bobby's class wanted to be a part of it. Bobby was the first to register, and his parents were relieved that someone approached them about tutoring kids in the neighborhood without them actually having to look someone up – and they and didn't bother asking to see his accreditation or certification either. They paid and trusted him. Charlie now ran a business out of his house. On top of that, he got other kids in the neighborhood into his novelty DVD's.

"Hey, you kids wanna watch a new DVD I got of botched hospital room amputations caught on camera? It's totally funny!" Charlie said.

"Yeah, we wanna watch that! Put that in!" The children he now took care of said in unison.

"You got it, dudes…"

## RICKY ROCKET'S BLUES

Ricky Rocket was born on an unusually cold night in June. The weather was predicted to be in the high 70's, with a slight chance of rain. Instead, what came was heavy hail and a whole lot of misery (the bad kind).

Ricky's mother, Larissa Rocket, was a failed blues singer. She had aspirations to find success as a musician, but her music lacked sincerity. Critics would call her kind of blues "unauthentic" and "contrived." Larissa had a very positive and content upbringing. Her parents were nurturing and loving, and would do anything for her. She had a very loving relationship with them. She took an interest in the complexity and poetry that sang out of her speakers after her father gave her first blues album to her on her twelfth birthday. She would attempt to mimic the craftsmanship in the songwriting, but was never able to excel. The experience devastated her – fueling her first authentic blues experience and material, but she took it too personally, and the failed album discouraged her from ever attempting to record or perform again.

The second kind of blues she experienced was Ricky's father walking out on her three months before Ricky's birth. He was a mechanic.

Larissa didn't want her son to share her fate. She wanted him to be an accomplished blues musician who could make any sap weep with his introspective lyrics and too-close-to-home melodies. She wanted him to gain the experience she unfortunately never did. However, in order to do this, she would need to be distant and cold towards Ricky so he could personally experience what the blues were about. The blues isn't just a genre of music. She knew that it was a feeling, a movement. She wanted her son to *feel* its authenticity – and who else would be best to teach that to him other than his mother? Larissa thought it would be a positive influence for her son to experience the blues until he became a worldly success. That was the only way she knew he'd succeed. She wanted Ricky to have 'real' material to sing about instead of sappy heartbreak songs, which were done to death by her. From the day of his birth up until he would become the greatest and saddest musician these seven continents had ever seen, she would give Ricky no love for his own good.

"Why don't you give me no love, mamma?" Ricky asked on his sixth birthday.

"Ricky, you were a horrible mistake from the get-go. You were always a waste of time. You ruined my body when you were in my oven belly. I always remember this on your birthday. You damn well don't deserve none of this," she responded as she threw out half of his stale birthday cake. "You don't deserve a great birthday, and you ain't my favorite son."

"Mamma, I guess you're right, I don't deserve none of this. I've been a bad boy these past six years. I ain't got nothin' to look forward to, I guess. I wish I wus your greatest son." He was Larissa's only son.

"That's my boy, Ricky – I mean, you're damn straight you ain't got nothin' to look forward to. Also, fer shit's sake, Ricky, why don't you pay more attention in English class? Shit, your grammar skillin' is goin' to shit. I want you doin' better in English and brush up on your writin'. Without you brushin' up on your writin' and articulation skills, you're gunna be as worthless as your daddy who never loved you. Now, repeat what I just said."

"Daddy never loved me."

"That's mah boy, Ricky, now go to your room and do your homework. I'll come in a little later to give you those birthday Stove Top Stuffin' crumbs."

Ricky walked to his room with his head hanging in shame. He found his toys placed on his pillow with their heads and limbs missing. Larissa had broken his action figures while he was at school that day. She had been waiting six years to do that. Upon realizing his toys were destroyed, Ricky walked to his mirror and stared intently at his reflection. He began to sob and whispered, "I got the blues…"

The next day at school, Ricky sat by himself scribbling on a napkin in the cafeteria. He was shy and self-conscious, afraid to socialize with other students. His mother would often tell him that no one would ever like him, and that everyone snickers behind his back, including herself. She often told him that if his own father didn't like him enough to stick around, why wouldn't anyone else do the same, too?

Classmate Sandra Starchaser had a crush on Ricky. She noticed that it was his birthday the day before on the calendar Mrs. Dragontail would keep in the classroom noting such days. She sat next to him to invite him to sit with her and her friends at their table.

"Hi, Ricky. Why are you always sitting by yourself? There are only two weeks before summer vacation, and you never ate lunch with anyone else. Come eat with us!"

"I don't deserve to," Ricky responded. "My mamma said I ain't good enough for people, and whatever mamma says is a fact."

"That's not nice, Ricky. My mother says everyone is unique in their own special way – and that all of us, together with our differences, would make a great omelet!"

"Your mamma don't know what the real world is like. I got it rough. I got the blues."

"Why do you have it so rough, Ricky?" She asked.

"Because my mamma never gave me no love."

"How doesn't she give you love? My doctor prescribes me seventeen hugs a day whenever I see my mom!"

"She don't give me nothin', and when she duz, she takes it away. Like yesterday. It wuz my birthday, and she broke all my toys. For my birthday last year, I was promised a clown, but got a dead goldfish. My mamma don't love me."

Sandra didn't know how to respond. She saw he was scribbling on a napkin. "Hey, whatcha writing?"

"This is a lil' song I wrote down. I ain't got the music. My mamma said that I should learn to play her guitar. She said she won't teach me how to play it, and that I'm too worthless to do anything else but play it, so I guess I'll learn to play it this summer now that all my toys are broken."

"Can I see this song you wrote?"

"Ok, but it's not gunna be good 'cuz I ain't worth poop."

"That is not true, Ricky! Did your mother say this to you?"

"No, she didn't say that."

"Oh, good, because I was about to say…"

"She said I ain't worth shit. I threw in the word 'poop' 'cuz I didn't wanna cuss in front of a girl."

Sandra was in shock. She barely spoke to Ricky, but was given all of this at once. It was too much for a six-year-old to handle. She started reading his song lyrics. They were the saddest words she had ever seen written down. She had never been exposed to so much pain, even though its structure was grammatically incorrect. But, the way he exposed himself in such a vivid way made her cry hysterically.

"This is the saddest thing I've ever read, Ricky…" Sandra said wiping the tears from her cheeks.

"I know, welcome to my life. Want a bite out of my Stove Top Stuffin' crumbs? They're stale and cold, but mamma said I don't deserve no warmth."

Eleven years later, Ricky was a seventeen-year-old high school senior. He taught himself guitar throughout the years, and made songs out of the lyrics he scribbled onto napkins. His mother occasionally broke his guitar strings so he'd have a clever blues song about writing a blues song, but then being unable to play it because he had no guitar strings, which would subsequently give him the music blues in the literal sense. She smelled Grammy when she thought of it.

Ricky improved his grammar, cadence, and articulation over the years. He also had himself a collection of fifty-two blues songs. He would play them to himself in his room, practically desensitized from the emotionally disturbing lyrics because he lived them time and time again. He once played a song for his mother.

"Ricky, I took a shit that sounded better when it plopped into the toilet water than that other shit you call your song," Larissa said after hearing it. "Speaking of which, I'm about to make a medley in the toilet now," she said as she walked to the bathroom. When she closed the door behind her, she looked at her reflection in the mirror and started to sob. It was the saddest song she'd ever heard. She was proud of her son.

Ricky followed the same routine at school since kindergarten. He'd sit by himself in the cafeteria, only this time with his guitar. Randy Billybaldwin was chosen to run the senior talent show, but was only able to sign four acts. No one had enough spirit to participate. He noticed Ricky would often have his guitar with him. Desperate, Randy sat next to him.

"Hey, your name's Ricky, right?"

"Yes sir, it is."

"You play guitar a lot?"

"Yeah, I play. I write my own songs, but I don't think they're good enough to play in front of other people."

"Nonsense, man. That's nonsense! You play in a band?"

"No, I don't really have any friends."

"You? Really? That's strange. I took you for a real rocker."

"I don't rock. I blue."

"What?"

"What I meant was that I sing the blues. I had a messed up childhood, so I write songs about my relationship with my parents who never loved me, and my sibling who didn't love me enough to want to be born."

"That's some deep stuff, man. That's Pacific Ocean deep, know what I'm saying?"

"I guess so."

"Listen, man, I'm not gonna beat around the bush. I need some acts for the talent show next week. I only have four signed up. One of which is myself. I, of course, will be showcasing my awesome standup comedy routine. I have a ton of awesome material. Some of it is real deep, like Pacific Ocean deep."

"Yeah, I've heard that one before," Ricky said.

"Listen, will you at least consider it? You said you think your material isn't good enough to play in front of other people. Well, how

do you know unless you've tried it? Take a shot, man. Just think if
Carrot Top never took his comedy act in front of the stage. Think
where we'd be now without him."

"I never really thought of it like that," Ricky said.

"So, do I have you in? Please, man? Please? I'm desperate here. I'll
even get on my knees and beg if I have to!" He said as he began to
kneel on the floor.

"Alright, I guess I'm in. If worse comes to worse, the experience
will be terrible and I'll have something else to write a song about."

"Excellent! You won't be sorry! By the way, it'll be four dollars to
sign up. I'm serious."

"Here," Ricky said as he pulled out the money and handed it to
Randy. "I wasn't going to buy lunch anyway. My mamma gave me
this money and said a bully would take it from me because I'm a
coward, small, and useless."

"Alright, man, I'll see you next Friday! Take care!" Randy said,
ignoring Ricky's last comment.

Ricky sorted through his songs that evening. He decided he'd
perform six of them. He told his mother about the talent show later
that week.

"They're allowin' you to play? Ricky, you ain't got no talent. What
you do got is the face of a fool and sucker thinkin' you're gunna
win," Larissa said.

On the day of the talent show, Ricky was set to perform: *Mamma
Raised a Fool; Daddy Shoulda Shot Me When I Was Born; I Ain't Got A
Face Worth Marrying; No More Pickles in the Refrigerator Blues; Kissing My
Storm Cloud; Daddy Shoulda Shot Me When I Was Born (reprise).*

The school auditorium was full, despite no one wanting to sign up
for the talent show. The event commenced with a dance number by
Rebecca and James Moondance. Then came a rap from Jonah
Dreidelspin. Ricky was scheduled to perform third. Randy prepped
him backstage.

"You ready, Ricky?"

"Yeah, but I know it'll be a big failure. I'll apologize to you right
now."

"Nonsense! You'll be great! I'll go on after you to let the heat
down with comic relief in case you bomb. I've got your back. Alright,
I have to go out and introduce you," Randy said as he ran out to the
stage.

"Give it up for Jonah Dreidelspin!" Randy said to the audience onstage. "Um, I think we need to call the roofers after that one. From this vantage point, I think he may have raised it a little. No, but seriously, that rocked my socks off – or shall I say rapped my boxers on. In case you're wondering, I'm kidding again! When does he stop? I don't even know! No, but seriously again, the next performer plays blues that would make Cookie Monster be like, 'This guy's bluer than my butt cheeks after a rough Saturday night!' No, but seriously, give a round of applause for Ricky Rocket, the original Blue Man Group!"

The audience cheered. Ricky walked onto the stage with his electric guitar and mini-amp.

"Good evening everyone. Please hold all jeers and bottles to throw at me after I'm done with my last song, thank you. Oh, and, uh, my name's Ricky Rocket."

Backstage, Randy immediately got upset, saying, "Hey, I'm the one who's supposed to be making jokes here…"

Ricky strummed his guitar once and looked into the audience to see his mother. She accidentally smiled at him, and he surprisingly smiled back. She immediately got nervous and thought that all her hard work for the past seventeen years was about to go down the drain, causing Ricky to lose his blues edge, so she immediately gave him a cold stare and the middle finger. The gesture wiped the smile off Ricky's face. He proceeded to play *Mamma Raised a Fool*.

Ricky performed his song with a passion he'd never felt before. One minute into the song, girls in the audience began to cry. After two minutes, the boys in the audience wept. Ricky's mother started to cry. She had never been more proud of her son.

Once the song ended, Ricky immediately went into *Daddy Shoulda Shot Me When I Was Born*. That got the mothers in the audience to cry. They were crying as hard as Sandra Starchaser did back in kindergarten after she read Ricky's lyrics on a napkin. When he played *I Ain't Got A Face Worth Marrying*, the whole audience and performers backstage were crying. The song expressed so much heartbreak and despair that it was unbearable.

The floor was slippery on account of all the teardrops falling on it. Ricky then began to play the very emotional and introspective *No More Pickles in the Refrigerator Blues*. The song made couples hug each other; fathers tightly grip their daughters; mothers glad to be alive and have a family.

By the time Ricky started playing *Daddy Shoulda Shot Me When I Was Born (reprise)*, he couldn't hear his vocals over the sound of the sobbing in the audience.

When he finished, he whispered, "Thank you for your time," and walked offstage. Randy hugged him as he arrived backstage and whispered, "I saw the embodiment of pain and sadness. It has your stature and structure. You are the saddest teenager alive, Ricky."

Randy wiped the tears from his face and walked onto the stage.

"Um, I'm here to perform a comedy routine..." he said.

"Shut your unfunny mouth and get a hobby!" A man from the audience yelled in a quivered voice. Tears continued to stream down the faces of children, students, and parents. No one had ever been exposed to such a melancholic voice revealing pain in such a melodic way. Audience members got up walked towards the exit, not knowing what to do with themselves. Ricky met his mother in front of the auditorium.

"Look whatcha done now, dummy," his mother said. "Your songs were so bad that you made everyone cry and go home. Now we'll never know who won the talent show. I bet it wasn't you, though."

"I'm sorry, mamma. I know I've always been a disappointment."

"You know, Ricky, you – " Larissa said before she was interrupted by a man who grabbed Ricky's shoulders.

"Son," the man said. "My name is Larry Sunfire. I'm the uncle of the Moondance twins who performed earlier tonight. Son, your music, excuse me..." He wiped tears from his eyes. "I'm sorry, but your music is beautiful and true. That fourth song you played was the saddest thing these ears have ever heard. Son, I would like for you to play my daughter Monica's sixth birthday party. We need an artist like you. You're not only a musician; you're a scribe, poet, and megaphone for beauty. I would like to also introduce you to someone who'll be at the party. Please come by. It's tomorrow, and I hope you're able to make it despite the short notice. What do you say?"

Ricky thought it over. He looked at his mother, who was biting her bottom lip.

"Sir, I would be delighted to bring my sad songs to your daughter's sixth birthday party," Ricky responded.

"Splendid," Larry said. "Here, son, here's my address. I will be paying you humbly for this. Please arrive promptly at three o'clock," he said as he wrote his address on the back of his ticket stub. "Here's my contact information. Thank you plenty, Ricky. I'll see you tomorrow."

Ricky's mother quickly turned away and smiled. She was proud of her son for finally being able to be something she was never able to accomplish; becoming a true, wanted blues musician. All of her hard work of bitterness, dejection, and despondency towards her son was starting to pay off.

"Let's go home, shit fer brains," she said to him.

"Yes, mamma..." Ricky responded.

At the Sunfire house the following morning, the stage was set up in the backyard for little Monica's birthday.

"Daddy," Monica said. "Will the magician and clown perform on stage with the horsie?"

"Monica," her father responded. "I've decided to cancel the magician and clown. I also told the rancher who brought the pony over earlier today to turn back and go home. I thought that the new act I booked for you would be more constructive. Art, darling, art. There are many forms of it. Art doesn't just consist of those hand tracings you do at school, where you draw a beak on your thumb and your hand magically becomes a turkey. No, Monica, art comes in many different forms. Last night, when I went to your cousin Rebecca and James' talent show, I came across the musical form of art, and I know that exposing it to you on your birthday will, both, introduce you to and enable you to be open to new forms of it. You will learn culture today, darling, and that is my birthday present to you. You'll thank me when you're eighteen and Harvard-bound. Happy birthday, Monica, and you're welcome."

Monica was confused. She began to cry. She was not going to be having the pony, magician, and clown after all. She ran to her room and slammed the door.

"Yes, that's the spirit, Monica! Life could be a son of a bitch! We, unfortunately, need to learn that the hard way," Monica's father yelled out. "Good thing we have people like Ricky Rocket in this world to expose us to life's depravities," he whispered to himself.

Ricky, drenched in sweat, walked through the backyard gate at three o'clock.

"Ricky!" Larry said. "Why are you so sweaty?"

"My mamma refused to drive me here. She said I wasn't worth the time and gas. Say, what's the stage for?"

"It's for you Ricky," Larry said. "Say, wait here for a minute, I want you to meet someone."

Ricky looked at the stage and at the party guests. He remembered his sixth birthday. He choked back the tears when Larry returned with a balding man wearing sunglasses.

"Ricky, this is the man I'd like you to meet. You may know his voice already," Larry said. "Son, allow me to introduce you to Ron. Ron here is a disc jockey over at WXBK."

"Pleasure to meet you, Ricky. Larry's told me a lot about you. I'm looking forward to hearing your stuff. Maybe, depending on how things go here, you could drop me a demo and I'll play it on my show. Are you a listener?"

"I think I know who you are," Ricky said. "Are you Rabid Ron?"

"Rockin' Ron, son, it's Rockin' Ron," Larry said.

"Oh, I'm so, so sorry. I'm sorry, Rockin' Ron."

"Not a problem, Ricky, happens all the time. Say, isn't it about time you got yourself ready up on stage?" Ron said.

"Yes, son, why don't you set yourself up? If you have any problems, just give me a holler," Larry said.

Ricky nodded and made his way to the stage. When he was set up, Larry got on stage and called for Monica.

"Monica, darling, this here is Ricky Rocket, and he wants to sing you some songs on this momentous day, your sixth birthday! Everyone, Ricky is a very talented blues musician I met last night at a talent show. Rebecca and James, you remember. Anyhoot, everyone please give a warm hand for Ricky Rocket!"

"Hi, everybody. Hi, Monica. Happy birthday. This song is for you," Ricky said. His first song began with the lines, "*No one ever loved me/No one ever cared/I wish the rain drops would wash me along with them to the gutter/Love me, mamma and daddy never dared...*"

Soon afterwards, everyone was in tears. Monica was crying on her birthday, Larry was crying on his daughter's birthday, Rebecca and James Moondance were crying on their cousin's birthday, and all of the guests were crying on the birthday girl's birthday. Ron broke out in hives after hearing the lyrics and guitar riffs. Ricky played a set of twelve songs. At the end of the twelfth song, Ricky ended by saying, "Happy birthday, Monica. May all your wishes come true."

Monica, covered in drool and tears, requested to be alone in her room with her thoughts. She felt an urge to throw away all of her possessions.

Larry and Ron approached Ricky as he was packing up.

"Ricky, son, you're an amazing songwriter. The way you galvanize us is truly revolutionary," Larry said.

"Ricky," Ron said while wiping tears off his cheeks. "Why are you so sad?"

"I never got no love from my mamma," Ricky responded.

"How about your father, son?" Larry asked.

"I never knew my daddy. From what my mamma said about him, he was a mechanic who was able to fix a Camaro, but not her heart."

"Poetry just floated out of your mouth, Ricky," Ron said. "I'll tell you what. Make me a demo, and I'll play your songs over at WXBK. Ricky, you have got talent. You've got it. I don't need to tell you a thousand times. You're going to be huge. Look at what your songs did to all of these people. Look at the children at this birthday party. They're all about five and six years old. Ricky, look at them. They're all in tears. Your music and words made them all feel an intense emotion. I *need* to play you on the radio. I have connections to big-time record producers. The name Ricky Rocket will be synonymous with sadness and depression. How could you experience so much sorrow and not kill yourself?"

"I dunno," Ricky said and shrugged his shoulders.

"Well, you'll probably have to sign a three-record contract or something to insure that you won't kill yourself after your first and second records if you suffer through this much heartache," Ron said.

Larry gave Ron a puzzled look after that comment.

"You could use the WXBK studio and equipment to record your music. Again, I need to play you. What do you say? Will you come in and record?"

"Sure, I guess so," Ricky said.

"Excellent. I want to do this as soon as possible. How does Monday sound? Will you come in on Monday after school?"

"Yeah, I guess I could do that," Ricky said.

"Great. Here, take my business card. Please excuse the tears. Let it be a mark of what you're capable of," Ron said.

"Ron's right, Ricky. You're poised to achieve greatness. My guests are going home. They don't feel like enjoying my daughter's birthday anymore. And you know what? I don't want to either, son, because I feel the pain and misery – you know, the bad kind – you went through," Larry said. "Here, here's a check for five-hundred dollars. Take it, and please make sure you go to the radio station on Monday to record the demo. Do you need a ride home?"

"No, no, sir, I wouldn't want to impose. My mamma always said that I would never have the right for anyone to go out of their way for me, and so I must abide by that. Thank you so much for the check. I am much obliged," Ricky said.

"Whatever you say, son, and thank you so much for doing this. It meant the world to me and to Monica, I'm sure of it. Have a goodnight."

Ricky walked home contemplating the record offer and whether to show up to the radio station on Monday.

"How'd the party go?" Ricky's mother asked when he got home.

"It went very well. Ragin' Ron from WXBK was there and said he wants me to record my music at the radio station he works at after school on Monday."

Larissa was so overcome with elation that she had the urge to hug her son. She restrained herself and said, "I don't care!"

She immediately ran into the bathroom and shed tears of joy. She didn't think the time was right to reveal the method to her madness after seventeen years. She told herself that she would wait until the big record deal came along.

Ricky received elevated attention that Monday at school. Girls smiled at him, boys nodded their heads in approval. Samantha Wildheart approached Ricky in the cafeteria during lunch.

"Ricky, sing me a sad song, please?"

"Uh, sure, what do you want me to sing about?"

"Just sing me any sad song," she said with a smile on her face.

"Alright," he said as he pulled his guitar out of his case. Samantha became giddy and clapped her hands while bouncing in her chair. Ricky started strumming his guitar, getting everyone's attention in the cafeteria. Doris, the lunch lady, even stopped short of serving the mashed potatoes. Ricky sang a song he wrote when he was six years old. It was the song that Sandra Starchaser read on a napkin years earlier. After he finished, Samantha hugged him and tried to say, "That was beautiful." It was jumbled in her hyperventilation.

"TTh-th-th-th-th-th-that wa-wa-wa-wa-wa-wa-was beau-beau-beau-ti-ti-ti-ti-ti-fffffff– " was all she was able to say before balling.

Everyone in the cafeteria began to cry. Ricky sang the saddest song that cafeteria's four walls had ever heard. Doris cried on the mashed potatoes as she served them.

Ricky went to the WXBK studio later that afternoon. He met with Ron and recorded ten songs in an hour. The songs came naturally to him, and making a mistake in a song he wrote was seldom. Ron told Ricky the same spiel he told him at Monica's birthday party in five different ways. He also promised Ricky that he would start playing his songs on the air during his popular radio program. Ron announced Ricky's song that evening.

"Ladies and gentlemen listening to Rockin' Ron's Rock Radio Evening on WXBK will remember this night. Tonight is equivalent to Ed Sullivan having The Beatles and Elvis for the first time on his show. Tonight, we'll take a break from the ball-crushing rock and roll we're known to play. I'm going to play you a song by an up-and-coming blues Michelangelo named Ricky Rocket. He sings the saddest and most tragic blues your ears will ever hear. Faithful listeners, this is a musical gift from Ricky, and I thank him for coming in to our studio earlier today to record these songs. America, get ready for Ricky Rocket, the saddest musician in the world! This song I'm going to play for you is called *Daddy Was Never There to Plant My Seed.*"

Ron played the four minute-forty-eight second song without further interruption. There was dead air after it finished. Ron was taken aback at how personal and tragic the music was. There weren't any listeners who immediately called the station after the song played. It took callers a few minutes to let everything sink in. After some time, listeners finally called the station crying, and a few of them got into car accidents after they lost their composure behind the wheel as they listened to Ricky's song on the radio.

Ricky and his mother listened to the show in the living room. Larissa started to cry. Ricky noticed.

"You did it, Ricky. You're finally on the radio, and soon you'll have important people calling you. I'm so pr —" Larissa said before cutting herself off. She remembered she promised herself that she'd open up after he struck the record deal. She thought Ricky was able to squeeze out a few more blues songs before then.

"You're so what, mamma?" Ricky asked. "What were you going to say?"

"I'm so practicing the way I'm gonna say *I told you so* when you fail miserably," she said, trying to cover up what she was actually going to say.

"Yeah, I guess you're right," Ricky responded.

The phone rang.

"Hello?" Ricky answered.

"Ricky, hi. This is Max Thunderbolt. I'm the founder and executive of Thunderbolt Records. I just heard your song on the radio. I called up Ron, and he gave me your number. I really like what I heard. If I were able to cry, I would. My tear ducts have unfortunately been sterile since my days in 'Nam. But that's a different story. Ricky, I smell talent in you. I even smell it over the phone. Ah, shoot, I may have made an ass of myself. Is this Ricky Rocket? I should really ask who I'm speaking to before I reveal so much information."

"Yes, this is Ricky."

"Oh, good! Anyway, Ricky, I'd like you to come by Thunderbolt Records. We're located in New York City. I'll fly you out here so we could talk in person. What do you say? Would you want to come out here and talk?"

"Oh, absolutely! When would I be able to fly out there?"

"I don't want you missing school, so how does this weekend sound? We'll fly you out here Friday night, and you could fly back home Sunday afternoon. We'll put you up at a hotel and provide you with a guide to show you around the city. You haven't lived since you've had a falafel from the Falafel King in the East Village. I'm not joking, don't have time to joke about stuff like that, so you know I'm serious."

"Sure! Wow, you really think I'm *that* good?"

"Ricky, seriously, you're an amazing musician. Hey, it's me. I know my shit. Excuse my French, but I'm Max Fucking Thunderbolt."

"Yeah, you're right, Mr. Thunderbolt."

"Call me Max. I'll have my assistant book your flight in the morning. She'll be calling you sometime this week to get everything in order. Let her know if you have any concerns or questions. Thank you, Ricky. You're going to be such a bright star that I should wear my sunglasses when I meet you."

"Thank you so much, Max. I'll see you this weekend!"

Ricky Rocket now realized what he was capable of. He needed

validation from someone as established as Max Thurnderbolt. He was finally convinced his music could affect people in a way that no one else's could. It was a force to be reckoned with. He needed someone like his mother or Max to boost his confidence.

"Mama, that was Max Thunderbolt of Thunderbolt Records! He's flying me out to New York to talk about a record deal!"

"Yeah, we'll celebrate that when you get it – but I'm prepared to hear all about you messing it up."

For the first time in his life, Ricky was unfazed by something his mother said. He nodded and went to his room.

The next day at school, Ricky walked the hallways with confidence. Students were complimenting him on a regular basis after they heard him on the radio.

"Ricky, that song on Rockin' Ron's show left me crying for three hours!" Said one person.

"Oh, yeah? Well, I was crying for three and a half hours!" Said another person.

"Yawn. I cried myself to sleep that night." Said a third person.

"I top all of you and am the biggest Ricky Rocket fan! I cried the whole night and morning, and if you look at my swollen eyes now, I'm *still* crying!" A fourth person said.

Ricky was letting the attention he was receiving from everyone he encountered get to his head. He looked at every student he passed and thought to himself that he could make him or her cry just through his words. He kept repeating to himself that he was talented because Max Fucking Thunderbolt said so. He saw star running back of the football team, Bobby Flash, with headphones on and tears flowing down his cheeks.

"Hey, Ricky, I'm listening to the radio, and your song just came on. How do you write such sad songs?" Bobby asked.

"My mamma gave me no love," Ricky said as if it were scripted and walked away. All Ricky could think about was going to New York City to meet with one of the most important people in the music industry.

Things began to change that evening, fueling a malevolent side as he listened to Rockin' Ron's show.

"That Ricky Rocket is a hack!" A caller said to Rockin' Ron over the air.

"Why do you say that?" Rockin' Ron asked.

"I could write sadder songs than that poser! I've *really* experienced the blues. My lyrics deal with pain, physical pain; blood, physical blood; broken bones, physical broken bones. Ricky Rocket only sings about emotional stuff. That's baby stuff. I sing about real street pain," the caller said.

"Oh, and what's your name?"

"The name's Charlie Blacklung. I'm sick of you guys claiming Rocket is the saddest musician in the world. You've played his songs repeatedly throughout the night and get back on the air sobbing like little girls. I'm calling Ricky Rocket out. I challenge him to a songwriting competition. You hear that, ya jerk? If you're really as sad as you say you are, then let's do this."

"Hold on a second. How do we know if your material is even sad enough?" Rockin' Ron asked.

"I'll tell you what, let me send you my music. I'm sure after you listen to it, you'll know why I'm the *real* saddest musician in the world."

"Fine, big shot, mail in your demo, and I'll play it on the air for the listeners to decide. Until then, you're getting the toilet flush," Rockin' Ron said and played his signature toilet flush sound effect before he hung up on the caller.

Ricky's classmates were concerned for him the following morning.

"Are you nervous about this new guy who says he's sadder than you are, Ricky?" Jeremy Stargaze asked.

"There is absolutely no way anyone is sadder than I am," Ricky said. "I'm able to make anyone cry."

Ricky anxiously listened to Rockin' Ron's show that night.

Rockin' Ron greeted his listeners in a somber tone.

"Ladies and gentlemen in radioland, I have heard quite possibly the saddest song I've ever heard. Charlie Blacklung's demo is very, very depressing, and it actually made this riff-raff disc jockey cry and feel the despair that Mr. Blacklung must have experienced. Without further ado, here is Charlie Blacklung's *A Brick to the Face, Daddy Even Strangled Me With A Shoelace*, on the Rockin' Ron show on WXBK."

The song did have some despair. Ricky felt the words in a way that his own never made him feel. When the song ended, Rockin' Ron addressed his listeners crying again. Callers were also calling in crying. There was one caller who called in laughter. It was Charlie Blacklung, challenging Ricky again to a songwriting competition. No longer able to take the ridicule and what he perceived to be a hack, Ricky called the radio station.

"We have Ricky Rocket on the air with us," Rockin' Ron said.

"Rocket, you going to accept my challenge? You never had it as rough as I ever did," Charlie said.

"Blacklung, I do accept your challenge, and I'm *very* aware that I could make more people feel my pain than you ever could," Ricky said.

"Sounding a little cocky now, aren't we, Rocket? Ok, Cinderella, your clock's about to strike midnight. How does tomorrow sound?"

"Totally fine with me. Max Thunderbolt even said I was the most talented."

"The guy from Thunderbolt Records? That guy's a hack, too," Charlie said.

"Max [beep] Thunderbolt, a hack?" Ricky said. Rockin' Ron was quick to censor him on the air.

"Ricky, mind you that we're live on the air. Please refrain from using foul language," Ron said. "Anyway, it's settled. If the both of you think that you could toy with people's emotions through your lyrics, I say come on down to WXBK. We could only have one saddest musician. We'll have a good old-fashioned song-off where, you, listeners out there in radioland, will vote on who the sadder musician of these two is! Tune in to tomorrow's Rockin' Ron's show to hear some of the saddest songs! Don't forget your Kleenex!"

Ricky and Charlie arrived to the studio the next day at the same time. Charlie was cordial with Ricky.

"Hi, Ricky. Hey, sorry for being such a dick on the radio last night. I gotta make a name for myself, 'ya know? Like, I respect your music and all, and it is a little sad, but I've had it rough, man, and I know how it really feels to be in the bottom of a shit pile," Charlie said.

"Yeah, your song was pretty sad, but Max did say I was the most talented," Ricky responded.

Ron interrupted their conversation.

"Alright, guys, here are the rules. You need to play original songs that are written on the spot here. You need to write them and then perform them. You can't use any material previously recorded; because in order to really have the blues, you need to absorb it in the moment and use those other fucked up experiences you've had to accompany it. You dig?" Ron said.

"Yeah, I understand, Rockin' Ron. By the way, your show rocks!" Charlie said.

"Yeah, I suppose I do understand, Rockin' Ron, but I also know this is a waste of time," Ricky said.

"Don't be so sure of yourself, Ricky Rocket," Charlie said.

"Alright, guys, shut up. The show's going to start in ten seconds," Ron said as he closed his eyes and took a deep breath. He got into character as soon as the 'on air' sign lit up.

"Good evening, night rockers! This is Rockin' Ron rockin' atcha with the hottest ball-crushing rock hits in this rockin' world, at this rockin' hour! Tonight is a special edition of the Rockin' Ron show. We have hometown legend after only three days, Ricky Rocket with us tonight! Also with us is another musical poet, Charlie Blacklung. Tonight's show includes a rock competition — or shall I say a blues competition? We're going to play you the hottest rock tracks while these blue kittens will write songs on the spot. After their songs are completed, they'll play them for you live on the air. It'll be up to you to decide who the sadder musician of the two is. First person to win majority out of eleven callers three times wins. Listeners, get by your phones and start listening. These two will start writing immediately after I press the play button on the song that I'm about to play. We'll be back in three minutes and twenty-three seconds!"

After Ron pressed play to begin the first song, he looked at the two blues musicians and screamed, "Go, begin writing now!"

Ricky wrote furiously and ferociously, while Charlie wrote ferociously and feverishly. When the song on the air finished playing, Ricky won the coin toss to perform first. He poured his soul into this song, about no one ever noticing him in school, no one ever taking the time to get to know him, and crying himself to sleep on his sixth birthday. It made Ron and his producer cry. Charlie's song was about the hardships of getting beat up every day after school, and telling his father in hopes of him doing something about it, but then getting beat up by him, too. While Charlie's song was sad, it lacked the genuine nature of Ricky's. The phone lines were opened. The first listener called sobbing, and said the sadder song belonged to Ricky. Ricky expected it. The second caller also voted for Ricky. Ricky's confidence grew. Then, something strange happened. The next six callers consecutively voted for Charlie, marking him as the winner of the first round. It infuriated Ricky. The anger he built up and buried in the past seventeen years was beginning to manifest itself. All his life, Ricky had suppressed his anger and resentment. He would let it out on paper. This time, however, he turned red and began to grind his teeth.

"Round one goes to Charlie Blacklung. Charlie, that was a pretty [beep] sad song. Excuse my language," Ron said. "Alright, the next track is five minutes and fourteen seconds. That's how long these two woeful musicians have to write another song, and the next batch of callers will decide who takes round two."

Ricky wrote so intensely that he broke his pencil. He quickly picked up another from the table. His second song was about how his only imaginary friend abandoned and left him for dead in the gutter, while Charlie wrote about an actual friend who really did abandon him up and leave him for dead in a real gutter in Cambodia. When the song on the air ended, it was Charlie's turn to go first. Ron got choked up as Charlie played it. He had been crying a lot these days, making his eyelids so swollen that he could barely see.

After Charlie performed, Ricky sang his song as slowly as he could. As he sang, he, himself, began to cry – something that had not happened in years. Ricky Rocket was crying along to his own music. When he finished, Ron was no longer able to see. His eyes were swollen shut. He needed his producer to come into the studio to handle the controls. The phone lines opened, and six consecutive callers voted for Charlie Blacklung again. Charlie just needed one more set of six votes to win.

"Charlie Blacklung, the guy who came out of nowhere and stole Ricky Rocket's thunder! Wow, everyone will be talking about you tomorrow," Ron said.

This took Ricky to an emotional point he had never reached before. He began to seethe, feeling betrayed by everyone. He felt betrayed by his mother, his unknown father, and everyone he had ever encountered – even Max Thunderbolt. He realized he internalized hatred. He thought he deserved better because he could move people in a way no one else could, and was owed better after living a life filled with humiliation, soul-crushing self-consciousness, and doubt. People pushed him to perform more, and even praised him. Now, Ricky saw them as turning their backs to him.

"Fuck them all," Ricky Rocket thought to himself. "If that's the way they want to do it, then I'll show them all. They'll all get what's coming to them."

The third song played on the air. It was six minutes and thirty-seven seconds long, giving Ricky ample time. He thought that since he was capable of toying with people's emotions and making them cry, he could make them do something else – something that made Ricky feel like they'd be getting what they deserved. He wanted to write a song that would make everyone who heard it want to kill themselves.

He wrote with a smile on his face. He knew the words that would make them do it. He subliminally placed messages for people to fatally harm themselves in various ways in the song. He remembered that he was Ricky Fucking Rocket, and that no one was a better songwriter than he was. He dug deep and hard to find a repulsive nature, and exposed it in a song, verse after verse. When the song playing on the air ended, Ron cued Ricky to perform.

"This song is entitled, *Blow Me A Kiss With A Shotgun*," Ricky said before he started. As he played his new song, everyone in the studio turned pale and began to stare at their palms. The song entranced even Charlie Blacklung. It gave people thoughts they had likely dreamed of in the darkest, most forgotten corner of their brains.

At approximately 9:27 p.m., the first person did it. Someone, after hearing Ricky Rocket's *Blow Me A Kiss With A Shotgun*, went to the roof of his apartment building and jumped off. Other people shot themselves. There were multiple incidents of people running onto highways and getting hit by oncoming traffic being reported. Rockin' Ron tried to find his way to the restroom to drown himself in the toilet, but ended up slamming against a wall because he couldn't see through his swollen eyelids.

There was dead air after Ricky finished his song. No one called in. People throughout the city were committing suicide, and the station's program director was trying to swallow an end of a stapler, hoping to choke on it. The show was taken off the air. Charlie Blacklung wondered which floor they were on, and whether he would survive jumping out the window. It wasn't until another twenty minutes when something happened. There was a frantic banging coming from the station's front entrance, immediately followed by a barrage of police officers in riot gear barging through the door. They made their way to the studio. They had earplugs in their ears and their guns drawn.

"Shut your fucking mouth and get down on the ground! I said get down on the fucking ground, and close your fucking mouth!" A police officer screamed. Ricky followed his instructions. He was handcuffed and duct-taped around his mouth.

Ricky was taken to the penitentiary. He remained duct-taped over his mouth in a jail cell. Thirty-eight people successfully committed suicide on account of Ricky Rocket's song that evening. He was charged with the murder of each of them by inciting their actions through his music. Ricky's mouth was considered a lethal weapon.

It turned out that he really did have a special power. No one had ever heard sadder songs than those of Ricky Rocket's. It was later discovered that Charlie Blacklung's songs weren't genuine. He had a team of sixteen people, all with Ph.D.'s in English and Poetry from Oxford, write the lyrics for all of his recorded songs and the ones he performed in the studio. He snuck in the lyrics sheet under his sleeve, but Ron's eyes were so swollen that he wasn't able to see the sheet unfurl before them during the competition. Charlie's cohorts figured out a way to rig the phone lines so their calls would go through before other callers, and voted for him. They called with tears in their eyes that were incited by Ricky, but voted for Charlie.

Ricky's balled-up anger finally exploded on live radio. Larissa Rocket was not one of thirty-eight people who had successfully killed themselves, but she did feel responsible for driving Ricky to a terrible and horrific extreme. He would end up held in solitary confinement.

Ricky was seen as threat to anyone who could hear his words. People around town had something new to cry about because they would never again hear the sad stories Ricky sang about. WXBK was prohibited from playing any of Ricky Rocket's songs. However, a number of tribute bands formed soon after to continue Ricky's short-lived legacy – an angst-ridden renaissance often referred to as the Ricky Rocket Revolution. Ricky Rocket, himself, had almost reached the top of, both, his dreams and his mother's. He had to learn the hard way of what he was capable of. He now had more than enough time to write the saddest blues songs no one would ever hear.

## NO ONE WILL LOVE YOU AS MUCH AS I NEVER DID

"What are you trying to say? I don't understand. You can't be doing what I think you're doing. No, it can't be! This can't be happening to me! Please tell me you're joking or that this is an awful nightmare! I know you're joking! You've got to be joking? What do you mean this is why you find me boring? So? You did what? To who? Jimmy? When? It's been ongoing for the past three months? You can't be serious. Please tell me you're not serious. I'd rather hear that you gave me an STD than this! Are you recording this conversation? You're doing me a favor? How is this any favor to me? What? You do realize today is what would have been our two-year anniversary, right? You called me to drop this bomb as I was getting ready to go to your apartment. I'm holding the bouquet of flowers I bought you! I'm holding them – for you – as you're telling me this! I need to go to your apartment to talk to you about this in person!

What? What do you mean I can't? No, this can't be true! Well, tell him to leave! Yeah, tell him I say, 'fuck you, too,' and that I could hear everything he's saying in the background! That son of a bitch! I'm going to kill him the next time I see him! So what if he knows jiujutsu? Ursula! It's been two years! This is how you're going to drop the ax on me? But, I love you! I love you so much! We're destined to be together! It's fate! Your name isn't Ursula and mine isn't Steven for no reason. Together, our initials spell 'us,' and that is what makes *us* so special! Alright, alright, very mature. Are you done now? Really? How so? No, I mean it. Please humor me. Because I want to know, that's why. Yes, I really want to know what makes me a loser. Because I trusted you? What? I can't believe you just said that to me! It's totally disgusting! Why would I want to know that you made out with me an hour after you blew another guy and didn't wash your mouth before we kissed? Well, it's not funny to me – it's not funny to me at all! How could you? How dare you! I'm out of line? You bitch! I'm so sorry. I was out of line by calling you that. I know. I know I could be childish sometimes. Please stop impersonating me for Jimmy's amusement. And please stop telling him I asked you to stop impersonating me. Ursula! Fine, fine. I'll admit it's my fault. Is that what you want to hear? Whatever I did, I'm sorry. It doesn't matter that you've been cheating on me for a year and a half. It doesn't matter that I basically tasted another guy when I kissed you that one time. Please, let me to pick you up so we could enjoy this day. Why? Because I love you, that's why. Stop laughing! Hello? Hello?"

Steven was dumped. He and Ursula had been 'dating' for the past two years, but he just found out that she had been cheating on him since their fourth month into the relationship. Her ex-personal trainer Jimmy had been sleeping with her for the past six months. Before Ursula cheated on Steven with Jimmy, she cheated on him with Mark, Dan, Bryan, Kelly, Jasmine, and Keanu Reeves. Ursula met Jimmy at a bar.

"I gotta drain this baby outta me," she said one drunken night as she barged into the men's room at a local dive bar as Jimmy was at the urinal.

"But, there aren't any stalls in here, only urinals," Jimmy said.

"I don't give a shit," she said as she dropped her pants and squatted over the urinal next to him. "You're cute. Why don't you come over here and swallow my tongue?"

"Sure," he said as he took the gum he was chewing out of his mouth and put it in her hair. It was the strangest drunken sex in a restroom since the time Abraham Lincoln had a one-off with a local prostitute in Illinois in 1847. She referred to him as her ex-personal trainer ever since.

Steven was at the bar that night, too. However, he stood by the Buck Hunter arcade and sipped on a Blue Hawaiian as he waited for his then-girlfriend to come out of the restroom. Most would wonder why Steven put up with the obvious fact that Ursula was in a constant state of infidelity. The truth of the matter is that Steven was one of the most oblivious men in the history of relationships. He thought he and Ursula would most likely marry someday. They were a well-liked couple on the days she was faithful to him. When news broke of their breakup, Steven looked to be consoled by his friends. He immediately went to his friend Chris' apartment after his phone conversation with Ursula.

"She dumped you?" Chris said in disbelief.

"Yeah, she totally ripped my heart into shreds," Steven said.

"You've got to get her back, Steven! Get her back!"

"She's already seeing another guy. It's that guy Jimmy, her ex-personal trainer who stayed at her place for two weeks to keep her company while I went to visit my folks in Florida. And here I thought it was just a nice gesture. He even wore my Bugle Boy jeans…"

"Is it serious with him?" Chris' wife Terri asked.

"I don't know. I don't think so," Steven responded.

"You know, I did see this coming," Terri said.

"Really? You knew she was cheating on me?"

"Steven, no offense, but you're in the wrong here," Terri said.

"What?" Steven said incredulously. "She broke up with me – and cheated on me!"

"I see Terri's point," Chris said. "How did you handle it when she told you?"

"I tried to get her back. I asked if we could talk about it in person."

"Oh, bad move. You totally messed up. Are you that dense in the head, Steven?" Terri said.

"What?"

"Dense in the head, idiot. She asked if you were dense in the head," Chris said as he pointed to his head.

"I heard what she said, but I don't understand where this is all coming from," Steven said.

"Steven, I've known you for about fifteen years, and I could honestly say that you screwed up every single of the two relationships you've been in," Chris said.

"That was phrased awkwardly, honey," Terri said to Chris.

"I know. I just wanted to say it in a way that gave the illusion that Steven has been with many women," Chris said.

"I get it now. That's very funny, dear," Terri said and chuckled.

"But, you guys…" Steven said before being interrupted by the phone ringing.

"Hold that thought," Chris said as he picked up the phone.

"Hello? Oh, hi, Ursula! How are you doing? Oh? Why are you crying? Yes, I know. I know. He's right here. Oh, you poor thing. I know you dumped him. It must have been so hard for you, I know. You are *so* brave. Jimmy did what? Oh, totally. Yes, I know. Good thing he left or else Terri and I would have had to shown him a thing or two. Ha! Yes, you're right! Well, stay strong, dear. I know, I know. Well, if you need anything, don't be afraid to be a bee and gimme a buzz, alright? Talk to you later, hon. Bye," Chris said and hung up. "Steven, get the fuck out."

"What?" Steven said.

"You've put this woman in enough of a state. Do you know how hard and brave it was for Ursula to collect the courage to break up with you and admit how unfaithful she was to you? She's as brave as a young, vibrant Susan B. Anthony and Maya Angelou rolled into one. And here you are, crying like Little Judy falling off her bike and scraping her knee. Get the fuck out, Steven. This here is Ursula Country. She's welcome here, you're not, get out."

"But…" Steven said.

"Steven, you heard my husband! Get the fuck out of our apartment!" Terri screamed.

"You guys are terrible friends," Steven said as he stormed out.

Steven didn't know what to do with himself. He knew that he had to be distracted in order to stop thinking about his situation. He was too gullible of a man to be involved with a woman like Ursula. A woman like her would eat him up, put her fingers down her throat in a bulimic fit, throw him up, and then suck him back up again with a straw. It was the second major heartache he had ever experienced. His first serious girlfriend, Paige, never reciprocated her love or affection. She chose her career over Steven, and moved to Chicago after a job opportunity arose.

"So, you're not going to reconsider this at all? Not for the sake of us?" Steven asked Paige at the airport before she boarded onto her plane to Chicago.

"Nope. Later, dude," she responded as she walked to the terminal.

She now had a kid and was married to a man she didn't love as much as she should have, but Steven didn't know this. He was distraught for months after their breakup, but forgot about her after he met Ursula. Ursula used to live down the hall from Steven's apartment. She gave him something he craved out of any living person, let alone any woman – attention. What he didn't notice, though, was that she showed a lot of guys even more attention.

One day, after Steven walked down the hall back to his apartment from Ursula's, the Dakota Brothers waited in the hallway maintenance closet until he closed his door. They then popped out of the closet and prepared to sandwich her like rye on ham. No, seriously, it was a gross sight. I mean, even the ceilings were stained after that night. She had since moved to a different apartment complex because she couldn't think of any more innovative ways to hide the other men she was sleeping with while living down the hall from her boyfriend.

Distraught after what happened at Chris' apartment, Steven reached out to his brother, Ben.

"I don't know who else to turn to. You're the only one I could talk to these days," Steven told Ben over the phone.

"What happened, Steven? Are you alright? Why don't you come over? I'll set up a bed for you on the couch," Ben said.

Ben was concerned when Steven arrived at his house. His younger brother looked pale, and his face was covered in tears.

"What happened to you? Tell me. You've got me worried," Ben said.

"Ursula dumped me…"

Ben closed his eyes and took four deep breaths. He hugged Steven.

"Are you serious?" He whispered into Steven's ear.

"Yes, unfortunately so…"

"What did you do?"

"I didn't do anything. She cheated on me and dumped me."

"She cheated on you? So what? It doesn't mean anything – just that she doesn't take the relationship as seriously as you do. There is nothing wrong with that, Steven, nothing."

"But, she cheated on me…and she dumped me…"

"Steven, sometimes you're going to have to fight for what you want. Do you want her back?"

"I don't know. A part of me does, but a bigger part of me thinks that I'm a sucker."

"Then, you've answered my question. You're a big fucking sucker. I always knew you were a sucker. I can't believe you forced her hand to dump you. Surely, you must have done something to merit her actions. I feel so sorry for her. What possessed her to do such a thing to my kid brother? I remember when you and I were little. You always wanted to play with those little toy trucks."

"What does that have to do with anything?"

"It was a metaphor."

"A metaphor meaning what?"

"A metaphor meaning that you should get in that fucking truck and get the fuck out of my house."

"What?"

"You heard me. Get the fuck out before I punch you in your stupid-looking face. You've got a lot of nerve. I should kick your ass right now out of principle," Ben said as he shoved Steven out the door.

"What did I do wrong?"

"You know, that girl put up with a lot of your shit. You just sat there whenever I saw the two of you together. She likes to have fun, likes to be punched in the face – just like one of the guys. I could only imagine the shit she had to put up with. She's like a brave and vivacious Whitney Houston for having to put up with you for as long as she did."

"Ben, I'm your brother!"

"And that's unfortunate. You screwed up, big time. It's a good thing mom and dad moved to Florida, away from your bullshit. Now, there's the door. Mind the gap, bitch."

"*This* is bullshit, you know that? You're the brother of the year. I wish I was never born!"

"You're really going to go down that route? Seriously, at this age? Get out, you're so pathetic."

"I hope I never see you again!" Steven said as he slammed the door behind him.

"Same here, dude, same here..." Ben said as he looked at himself in the mirror next to the front door, curled his upper lip like Elvis, and winked at his reflection.

Steven didn't know where else to turn. He called his mother on his way home, hoping to be consoled by the person who's always done so in the past.

"Hello?" His mother answered.

"Hey, mom..."

"Steven, you don't sound like yourself. What's wrong, dear?"

"Mom, I need someone to talk to, and I don't know who else to turn to."

"Have you gotten yourself into trouble?"

"No, it's just that—" he said before a car screeching to a stop interrupted him. A large man got out of the car.

"You motherfucker! I'm gonna chafe my dick as I'm fucking those eye sockets of yours!" The large man said.

"Ted? Ted is that you?" Steven said.

"What's going on there, Steven?" Steven's mother asked over the phone.

"I have to go, mom. I'll talk to you later!"

"But, honey! I—" Steven's mother said before he hung up on her.

"Ted! What do you want?" Steven said as he panicked and ran away.

"I'm gonna fucking murder you in the first degree! There is no greater murder offense than the one in the first degree, and that's just what I'll be doing to you – first-degree shit! You and my sister are over!" Ted said as he ran after Steven.

"But, I didn't do anything to her! She broke up with me! She cheated on me!" Steven said.

"Doesn't fucking matter, Steven! You're dead! Fucking dead! Fuck yeah!"

Steven eventually ended up at the park. He pulled out his cell phone and called Ursula.

"Hello?" Ursula answered as she painted her nails.

"Ursula! Why's your brother coming after me? He's threatening me with murder – in the first degree!"

"Oh, I told him that we broke up. He totally wants to kick your ass. I'd stay away from him if I were you."

"Well, he found me alright! I didn't do anything to you! What did you tell him?"

"What? Are you serious? He said he wouldn't harm you. I thought he was serious this time," she said as she blew on the wet nail polish she had applied to herself. "I mean, I found it weird when he went over your house to look for you. He then asked where else you could be after he told me you weren't there. I told him I'd tell him on the condition that he wouldn't go after you. He agreed. So I told him you'd most likely be at your brother's house. I guess he lied to me."

"You really think so?" Steven said sarcastically.

Ursula faintly heard her brother yelling in the background.

"My poor sister is like a bold and incorrigible Eleanor Roosevelt! She was so courageous to break your fucking heart!" Ted yelled.

"Is that Ted yelling in the background?" Ursula asked.

"Yeah, it is!"

"Oh, that's cool," she said as she yawned.

"Ursula, why are you doing this to me? What did I do to you? Why won't you take me back?"

"Steven, do we have to get into this as my brother's chasing you? Besides, it's late."

"When would be a more appropriate time, then?"

"Fine," she said as she sighed. "What do you want?"

"I love you!" He said as he ran into the wooded area of the park.

"Really? After all I've put you through, you still love me?" She said in an annoyed tone.

"Yes, I do!"

"Fine, well, I'll tell you what. If you get out of this tangled, fucked up situation with my brother you got yourself into, then I suppose you could come over."

"Really? You mean it?"

"Sure. I have a heart and conscience. I'm not a cold-hearted bitch."

"No, of course not!"

"Yeah, see you when I see you," Ursula said and ended the call.

Steven crouched silently behind a row of trees. He heard Ted rustling through the leaves.

"Steven, buddy, I know I overreacted. I'm sorry. Why don't you come out so I could apologize to you?" Ted yelled.

Steven almost fell for it and came out, but then remembered that Ted was a good liar.

"Steven, seriously, buddy. I'm sorry. I know you don't have a car. I'll drive you home."

Steven stayed quiet and still.

"Fine! You're lucky it's dark out, you cousinfucker. I know where you live! I've slapped a little kid in the face before, Steven, so don't think I won't slap yours in a second! You're fucking dead! I hope a wolf or some shit eats you out there, asshole," Ted said as he walked away.

Steven waited a few more minutes until he knew the coast was clear. He exited through the opposite side of the park. It was a more roundabout way, but it insured that he wouldn't cross paths with Ted.

As he made his way to Ursula's apartment, Steven passed a restaurant he'd frequent with her. He stopped and remembered about the first time they ate there. Ursula didn't know where the ladies' room was, so she asked one of the male waiters. He walked her to her destination, and was nice enough to stay with her and walk her back forty-five minutes later.

A waiter inside noticed he was looking in. He opened the door.

"Sir, would you like to hear the specials of the day?" The waiter asked.

"No, no, thank you, though. I have to meet with my girlfriend – or shall I say ex-girlfriend – or shall I say my ex-girlfriend-possibly-soon-to-be-my-girlfriend-again?"

"It sounds like you have a busy night ahead of you," the waiter replied.

"You don't even know the half of it. She and I ate here a few times."

"Oh, yes? You look familiar."

"Yeah, Ursula and I –"

"Ursula! Yes, you are Ursula's boyfriend. Rafael never forgets a face! She has quite a reputation, that Ursula – or should Rafael say Ursul-uh-uh-uh-uh-baby-don't-stop-there-give-it-to-me-until-I-bleed-from-my-ears. At least that's what Rafael heard. She is a very popular lady around here," the waiter said. "And you two are no longer together? Carajo. She is as vibrant as a young, tenacious Oprah Winfrey."

"Yeah, that's what I sort of keep hearing. Anyway, I'm going to try to patch things up with her, so I should get back on my way. If things work out, maybe we'll both eat here tomorrow."

"Oh, please, yes. If you see her, let her know that Tito learned new back-butt tricks on the grill. She'll know what that means."

"Yeah, I will. I have to go. See you later."

"Rafael wishes you good luck!" The waiter said to Steven.

Steven wondered if there was any person Ursula had not slept with.

Once he got to her lobby, he buzzed her apartment, but she didn't answer until fifteen minutes later.

"Hello?" She asked through the telecom.

"Hey, it's me. Steven."

"What are you doing here?"

"You said I could come over."

"Oh. Alright," she said and buzzed him in.

They both sat down on her couch after he came inside.

"Ursula, don't do this. Please don't do this to us. We've been together for too long," Steven said.

"Steven, is this what you came here for?"

"Yeah, why else would I come over?"

"I thought you just wanted to talk about other things, like windsurfing, kayaking, elephant poaching – you know, stuff like that."

"Why would I want to talk about other things with you at this point?"

"I don't know. I feel so terrible."

"I do, too. Please take me back!"

"What?" She said with a disgusted look on her face. "No, not about us. I don't feel terrible about us. Jimmy said he doesn't want to see me anymore."

"Really? That's great!"

"Steven, grow up. I miss him. You have no idea how hung he was. Not being able to talk about this with you proves that you're not mature enough to see me."

"I'm sorry. You're right, I guess," he said, not wanting to agitate her any further.

He grew uncomfortable with the conversation, but thought he'd be on her good side if he listened, and therefore she'd be more inclined to take him back.

She continued, "Good. Now, where was I? Oh, yeah, so hung. Seriously. It's true what they say about black guys. His penis was like a public payphone receiver hanging off the hook, swaying from side to side."

"Oh, is that so?" He said.

"Yeah... it is..." she responded.

He stopped paying attention so he didn't have to hear the sordid details, but smiled and nodded throughout. She spoke for about twenty minutes, where she mimed various sexual positions and girth sizes with her hand, did a handstand, compared the girths of an oversized cucumber and a rolling pin, and eventually took her pants off.

"Well?" She asked.

"Well what?" He responded.

"Are you gonna take off your pants or what?"

"Huh?"

"Well, we can't fuck if your pants are still on."

"Wait a second. Are we back together?"

"No! Haven't you been paying attention to what I've been saying?"

"Of course I have! I'm just confused."

"I said that you told me you loved me over the phone earlier this evening."

"Yes, that's true. I remember that."

"Well, I haven't gotten laid in like four hours. And now that Jimmy left, it doesn't look like I'll get any tonight. So, since you love me, let's have sex."

"But, it won't mean anything."

"So? You love me, right? If you love me, it doesn't matter how I feel about you."

"What? That doesn't make sense, and it's not right. I love you! It's way more than just sex."

"Steven, I know that. It's not like I don't know what love is. I know the difference between fucking and loving. I've known the difference since I was eleven years old. Now, will you take your pants off?"

"No. I won't subject myself to this. I won't give you a pity fuck. I'm above that!"

Ursula began to laugh.

"You think *I* need a pity fuck?" She asked.

"Yes, why else would you want me to have sex with you right now, even though we're broken up? I'm not going to have emotionless sex with you, Ursula."

"So, you're not going to have sex with someone unless they love you?"

"Yes, that's correct."

"Oh, Steven," Ursula said as she laughed. "Steven, poor Steven. Look at me, honey. Look straight into my eyes and listen to what I'm going to tell you. No one will love you as much as I never did. So, it looks like you're never going to have sex again for the rest of your life."

Steven was taken aback by her comment. He stood up and walked out of the apartment without saying a word. He heard her laughing as he closed the door. He walked home and didn't care about the fallout that would come his way after this encounter. He kept replaying the experience in his head. It wasn't what he wanted to hear out of her mouth, but it was what he needed to hear, regardless of how much it hurt him. While on his way home, he got a call from Chris. He thought Chris came to his senses and was calling to apologize after what happened earlier that evening.

"Hello?" Steven answered.

"You wouldn't even give her a pity fuck? Seriously?" Chris said.

Steven hung up on him and decided he needed to take a break.

He booked a much-needed vacation a few days later. He decided to travel to Italy. He had never visited the country before, and wanted to gain new, independent experiences. On the plane, he was seated next to an attractive girl whom he eventually befriended on the flight. They shared a few things in common, and small talk eventually turned into an engrossing conversation. Steven found himself very attracted to her. She took his mind off of Ursula and the mental duress she caused him.

"So, where are you going in Italy?" He asked the girl.

"Oh, a lot of places. It's actually the first time I've ever left the country," she said. "I'm going to stay in Rome for a couple of days and explore it. After that, I'd love to see the gorgeous art and architecture in Florence, and it's always been a dream of mine to take a gondola ride through the canals of Venice. I'm going all-out while I'm there."

Steven was completely smitten with her. He had also never left the country prior to the trip, and was also traveling alone with the intention of exploring Rome, Florence, and Venice. He thought this was fate finally sending him someone who would love and appreciate him.

He started to doubt Ursula's influence and hold on his life. He was confident he'd find someone who would love him; wouldn't choose her career over him; wouldn't cheat on him with multiple men, women, or farm animals – even though it hadn't been proven that Ursula had committed such an act, but it had been strongly implied in the past. He decided to take the plunge by being direct with his new acquaintance and seeing where he would land.

"Would you like to explore the country together? I mean, since we're both going alone and share a lot in common. We should definitely take this trip together," Steven said.

She gave him a smirk and nonchalantly said, "I have a boyfriend."

"That's okay," Steven replied.

"No, that means I'm not interested in taking this trip with you once we land."

"Fair enough," Steven said and looked out his window in silence for the remainder of the flight.

## YOU'RE PRETTIER IN THE DARK

Welcome to the nightmare that is my life. I can't believe I'm going to divulge information to you. If you read this, I will surely kill you and then myself out of embarrassment. The past seventeen years of my life have been nothing short of pathetic. I can't stand it anymore. I'm writing to you as I sit in detention after an altercation involving mega-bitch Sally Marshall. I can't wait until she contracts a sexually transmitted disease and bleeds to death out of her vagina or chokes on her vibrator – whichever comes first. I don't know why I'm even writing this. We're not allowed to talk, but Mr. Bryan said we could do our homework. Too bad I was stupid enough to do it during study hall. Why is it that when I actually do something productive, there's always a better payoff to do it at a later time? I've never kept a diary, so I guess this could sort of make up for it. Who's going to read this, anyway? I'm hiding this note, waiting until you find it. It's too late for you to escape since you've read this far already. I'm on my way now to kill you and then offing myself. It'll be a gift from me to the *both* of us, trust me. I'm sure that since you're presumably a student at this fine institution, you know what a bitch and slut Sally Marshall is. She is the town whore. She's pretty much tasted every guy — EVEN YOUR DAD, I bet. Don't judge me as a pessimist or cynical. I'm normally not. I mean, I do come from a very dysfunctional family. On top of that, I've met my share of oddities and people who would have benefited from being aborted. I can't wait to get away from all of them this fall when I go away to college. I need a change of scenery. I need to meet new people and avoid others – like some boys in my life. I'm not saying I'm the be-all-and-end-all, but I do need to avoid some boys. Ugh, who am I kidding? I'm referring to only one. I'm not the most gorgeous girl in the school, but let's just say that the guys who show interest in me could be child molesters just itching to take the long way home in order to pass the playground – especially the oddity I'm referring to. I also need to get away from whores like Sally. As certain as I am my period is the third week of every month, I'm certain I saw her masturbate after gym in the shower one day. She'll deny it, but I totally saw her. She said it was 'an itch,' but let's not play stupid. Enough with the introductory mumbo-jumbo. I won't give out any last names besides Sally Marshall's because you may have already heard of her. Just ask your little brother. My name is Alexis. As I alluded to a few lines up, I'm a senior, and it's the third week of May, so figure out why I'm so pissed.

Where should I start? Well, parents are usually any therapist's go-to topic, so I guess I'll start there. They're one of those socially awkward couples that don't do anything with other people, but fight with each other all the time. I hope I don't turn out to be like them.

"Alexis, why don't you start wearing makeup more often?" My mother asked me once.

"I don't feel like wearing it. Are you saying I'm ugly?" I responded.

"No, sweetie. All I'm saying is that you could enhance your beauty a little. Is that such a mean thing to say? I haven't heard any boys calling to speak to you. That must say something…"

She could be a bitch, I know. She's condescending to everyone – especially to my dad. They've almost gotten divorced a number of times, and have gotten separated even more than that. The irony is that they're both divorce lawyers. My father and I don't really have much of a social life with each other. I think it must have started about seventeen years ago when he saw I never sprouted a penis. Since then, we've sort of hit a rough patch. He gets me what I want for my birthday, which is cool. I don't know whether he does this on purpose or what, but he always leaves the price tag on the gifts he gets me. He usually does half-assed attempts to blacken the price out with a marker. Once, he 'accidentally' blackened the tag with a highlighter. My parents make good income. As I mentioned, they're both lawyers. But, what do they do with their wealth? They decide to send me to this school. I'm pretty certain the kid who has the locker to the left of me has a gun hidden in there, while I know that the one to the right has a machete. It's too bad they're in rival gangs.

This school is a mess. People like Sally Marshall are the princesses of the hallways. They're so gross. They have no regard for other people. I remember meeting Sally like it was yesterday. We've been in the same class since the third grade. I don't know how it happened, but she turned into a fake bitch who'll stab you in the back to further herself. She did it to me. We used to be friends. Then, one day we decided to shoplift perfume from Macy's. She planted some items in my bag without me knowing in an attempt to impress some other kids. Being the butt of her joke totally screwed me. The kids she was impressing were 'cooler' because they were sophomores while we were freshmen. I got into so much shit for that. She started hanging out with that new clique and acting like the asshole she is today.

"Hi, Alexpiss," she cleverly said in front of her new friends.

"What the fuck is your problem? You do realize I'm grounded for like three months because you, right?" I said.

"Sorry it happened, but you had to see the look on your face. It was so worth it," she said.

"Fuck you. Don't you ever talk to me again. You're no longer invited to come over my house to braid each others hair," I said, and then her and her minions laughed at me. I walked away, but heard her say, "Bye, Alexpiss, hope your daddy doesn't have another shitfit."

She continued a story she was apparently in the middle of telling her friends before I showed up, "So, anyway, I was like, 'Joey, fine, I'll suck it, but I'm *not* gonna like it!'"

"You showed him, Sal," one of her friends said.

"You definitely stood your ground by saying that," said another friend of hers.

With Sally not my friend anymore, I was running low on them. The truth of the matter is that I didn't have any other than her. When she realized she was actually attractive and got the attention of older kids, she dropped me faster than an unwanted baby on prom night. I had no choice but to start hanging out with my cousin. He's pretty cool. We still get along and all. He was the coolest twelve-year-old I'd ever known. We've always been into the same things and all. He was, and possibly still is, too into Star Wars and sci-fi for my liking, though. I didn't really like it, but it'd give me an excuse to go out on weekends. I started going to Star Wars conventions with him.

The freak show at a Star Wars convention is totally worth going to them. My cousin would usually dress up as an ewok. I thought it was kind of pathetic, but he said I was whenever I'd go and wouldn't dress up. The truth of the matter is that even in these geeks' eyes, I was pathetic because I was the only one who didn't dress up. I couldn't, and still can't, fit in anywhere. Anyway, we went to one every six months. I'd sit myself at the food court and be awestruck by these human specimens as they walked around. Some of them were as old as my parents. So, anyway, there's a point to this. One time when I was there, I was approached by this 'thing.' This 'thing' was a person dressed as Yoda – you know, the Jedi master and shit. He had the pointy ears on, green makeup, and all. I couldn't help but laugh in his face at first.

"Hi, so whatcha doing here with all these dorks?" He said as he scratched his left arm. "This green makeup really gives me a rash."

"I'm here with my cousin…he's twelve. How old are you?" I said as I giggled at how stupid he looked.

"Old enough, sweet stuff. Damn, I'm itching all over, even on the back of my neck," he said as he started scratching the back of his neck and pulled it out. I'm convinced the whole rash gimmick was an anecdote to reveal it. He pulled out a rattail. What guy grows a rattail this day in age unless he's openly dating his thirteen-year-old sister?

"I'm sorry, did that scare you?" He asked, referring to his rattail.

"Oh, my, it is big, and a little intimidating, but I think I'll be alright," I said.

"Yeah, get that all the time. I have it 'cuz I'm a padawan," he said.

"Is that a town in Puerto Rico?" I asked.

"No, but that is funny," he said in a condescending tone as if I should feel bad for not knowing what the fuck a padawan was.

"A padawan is a Jedi in training," he said. "I'm learning from the master."

"I thought you were supposed to be Yoda. Isn't he a Jedi master?" I asked.

"You're missing the point!" He said with a tone of annoyance. "This convention is a charade. It's all for fun, for games, for the kids. Real life is real life, and I'm really a padawan."

"What's you name?" I asked him. I was totally intrigued by this freak.

"Do you want my Jedi name or my mortal name?" He asked.

I was tired of playing games.

"Forget it, I don't care," I said.

"PIPER! My name is Piper!" He said in desperation.

"Well, hello, Piper. My name is Alexis."

"What brings you here with these dorks and kids, Alexis? You're a good-looking girl."

"Thanks....I'm here with my cousin. He's a lot younger than you."

"Oh, a novice. Well, if he needs to learn the ways of the force, he could place his trust upon me. I promise I won't sway him to the dark side...much."

I was tired of the Star Wars jargon.

"So, yeah, my cousin ran off, and I need to find him. There are a lot of weirdos and child molesters with a lot of promise lurking around here. I'd better go," I said.

"How about we look for him together?" He said. "I know this place pretty well. We'll find him in no time."

Now, being that I was, and am, new to the art of being flirted with or hit on, I originally thought this guy was generally creepy, and not really trying to rub up against me – which he did while looking for my cousin.

"Sorry, this is a big cloak. Even too big for me..." He'd say whenever I felt a rub on my ass. This guy was *way* creepier than I originally thought, now that I think about it in hindsight. He knew the area pretty well, though. We found my cousin pretty quickly by the vending machine. Typical.

"Peter, there you are. Don't you ever stray off like that again without telling me where you're going," I said to him a little pissed because if he hadn't run off, I wouldn't have had to spend more time with Piper.

"I think it's about time we left," I said to the both of them. "I'll call my mom to come pick us up."

As I stepped away to use the payphone, I looked back and saw my cousin standing with Piper. I got uncomfortable, so I walked back and pulled Peter's hairy ewok sleeve towards me.

"Maybe it'd be a good idea if you came with me," I said to him, not taking my eyes off Piper. "Well, it was nice meeting you, Piper. We'll see you again at the next Star Trek convention."

"WARS! STAR WARS!" He exclaimed.

"Right…" I said as I pulled Peter away.

I proceeded to call my mom. She answered the phone after sixteen rings. She sounded drunk.

"Hello?" She answered.

"Mom, it's Alexis. Peter and I are done here, could you come pick us up?"

"Alexis! Darling! I can't come get you! I think I may have drank a little too many, if you know what I mean."

"Fine, how about dad? Could he come get us?"

"I'm afraid your f-f-f-father no longer lives here. I kicked him out."

"You what? What is that, like seven times in two years? I find it difficult for him to not want to come home to such a winner like yourself," I said sarcastically.

"I know, right? Your father is what us older women refer to as an asshole. Do you know what an asshole is?"

"I think I get the point."

"Yes, if you look at the family portrait in the living room, you'll find a picture of your father. That is the definition of 'asshole.' When are you driving home? I've made breakfast for you."

"Mom, first of all, I don't have a license. Second of all, we ate breakfast earlier. And third of all, you don't cook. What's your problem?"

"My problem is that I married your father, an asshole."

"So, yeah, um, I guess I'll take the bus."

"Yes, dear, that sounds wonderful. I'll see you next Wednesday, then," she said before she hung up.

"Shit..." I said as I sighed. I looked at my cousin and was pretty sure he was completely naked under his costume, so I couldn't ask him to take it off when we left the convention center. I really didn't want to take public transportation, but we had no other option.

Sitting on the bench at the bus stop, I felt embarrassed, and not just because I had my cousin next to me dressed as an ewok, but because of the joke my life was. I had resorted to going to those fucking Star Wars conventions because I didn't have any friends. My parents were insane, and my mother was on that slippery slope of becoming an alcoholic. What did I have going on for myself? Don't try to respond to that question, because you won't be able to come up with an answer. Anyway, as I was thinking I couldn't sink any lower while waiting for that bus, a station wagon drove past us, stopped, and reversed. The front passenger window rolled down. I was ready to be pelted with eggs or paintballs. I saw Piper stick his head out of the window and exclaim, "That's them, mom! I told you I made friends today! Alexis! It's me Piper! You need a ride home?!"

I was embarrassed enough as it was, so why not sink lower? I accepted, and my cousin and I got into the back seat. Piper's mother didn't say a word. Not one word. Piper did all the talking.

"So Alexis, did you like the convention today? I think it's definitely getting too commercial. Don't you agree, ewok?"

"I guess..." I said. My cousin knew better. I wish I had pretended to fall asleep like he did.

"Do you listen to music, Alexis?"

"Sometimes..."

"Well, you have to check out Metallica in case you haven't already. They're like the greatest band in the world. They rock so hard. They have the coolest designs. I'm thinking about getting a tattoo of one of them. Pretty cool, huh?"

"I guess. I don't really know too much about them. Say, thanks a lot for the ride, miss," I said to Piper's mother. She said nothing in response.

I tried looking out the window to block out everything I had gone through that day, but Piper made it virtually impossible.

"Did you see that dork at the convention dressed as Mace Windu? I mean, he was a white guy! Hello, Earth to the third moon of Tatooine! Mace Windu is black!" I heard shit like that throughout the trip. It's still the longest twenty-minute car ride I've ever taken.

When we got to my house, Piper got out of the car and opened the back door for me and my cousin. It was small, nice gestures like that I really longed for. No one was that nice to me anymore. I started thinking that this guy wasn't so bad after all. He was definitely a dork, but maybe he was friend-worthy. I mean, I thought my cousin was the coolest kid I knew, and he's into Star Wars, so maybe this guy was cool, too.

"You want to hang out sometime?" He asked me.

"You know what, sure, why not?" I responded.

"Oh, great! What's your number?" He said as he quickly pulled a pen from the glove compartment. He wrote my number on his forearm after I gave it to him.

"Have a great night and awesome tomorrow, Alexis!" Piper said to me as he skipped and clicked the heels of his feet together in midair as if he were Fred Astaire before getting back into the car. Piper's mother then peeled off.

Peter and I watched television until ten o'clock. His mother came by and picked him up. When he and his mother left, mine came crawling into the living room from her bedroom.

"What the fuck was that noise? Anyone in here?" She asked.

"No, mom, it's just me," I responded.

"Oh. Did you hear that your father just packed up his things and left? I mean, the audacity!"

"That's funny, because you told me you kicked him out."

"Oh, you're such a smart girl! You're also a fucking brat!"

"Mom, it's ten o'clock, I think it's time for you to go to bed."

"Don't tell me what to do. I tell you what to do, and I am ordering you to put on more makeup. Didn't I tell you this a while ago?" She said as she turned off the lights. I turned them back on.

"Alexis, don't turn the lights on, honey. You're prettier in the dark," she said.

"Fuck you," I said to her as I stormed into my room and slammed the door.

I was so sick of the shit I was going through. My best friend at the time ditched me, my mother was a drunk, my father was nowhere to be found, and the only person who had ever shown any iota of interest in me most likely stared at his penis in the mirror. I needed something new in my life. I was interested to see what this guy Piper was really all about. Coincidentally, he called me like five minutes later.

"Hi, is this Alexis?"

"Hi."

"Hey, this is Piper. Remember? I'm the guy from the Star Wars convention whose mom drove you home!"

"Hi."

"If you're not doing anything tomorrow, I'm free. I finished all of my homework, and so my mom said I could have a fun day. What do you say I ride my bike to your house and then we go to the mall or something?"

"Sure. I hear there's a new arcade there. Want to check it out?"

"Eh, I don't care much for arcade games, but we could do other things at the mall!"

I was totally thrown off-guard by that. How could *this* guy not be into arcade games? This was the Jedi apprentice who dressed up as Yoda as a hobby, right?

"Alright, we'll see where the day takes us. When do you think you'll be over?" I said.

"How about I show up at six-thirty?" He responded.

"Isn't that a little late? The mall closes at eight."

"No, I meant six-thirty in the morning."

"Oh… No, I don't think that would work either. I'll be asleep. How about we do normal people time and say around noon or one o'clock…in the afternoon?" I said as specific as possible.

"Sure…I guess…if you say so…" He said in a defeated tone.

"Hey, Piper, I have to go. I'm going to have some smoothies with my mom," I said as I heard my mother throwing up in the bathroom across the hall. "I'll see you tomorrow," I said and hung up.

It didn't matter that I hung up on him. I knew he'd come anyway. Even though someone being interested in me was foreign to me, I knew that I had free rein to do whatever I wanted when it came to this kid. I didn't bother checking up on my mother. The last thing I remember from that night was her vomiting, crying, and saying, "Oh, shit…"

My mother acted as if the night before never occurred in the morning. It was common, and I was used to it. Whatever mess she may have left on the bathroom floor was cleaned up, and of course, my father had come back earlier that morning. They patched things up. It was as if they eradicated everything that occurred – all the tears and swearing. Again, it was a common occurrence here. Anyway, I was getting caught up on my homework at around noon when I heard the doorbell ring. It was Piper with sunglasses on. He was wearing croakies with them. In case you don't know what croakies are, they're the laces that you attach to the frame of your sunglasses so that they are able to hang around your neck. I have nothing against them, except when they're neon green and you have a rattail. He showed up on his bicycle, like he said he would. My mother was thrilled to hear a boy was taking me out. I think she may have thought I was a lesbian until then.

"Hey, puma cub," he said to me as I opened the door. You know you're a loser whenever you refer to someone as 'puma cub.' I was beginning to resent my decision to hang out with him.

"Hi," I said. "Mom, I'm going out. I'll be back a little later."

"Wait a second, Alexis. Well, hello, there…" She said to Piper as she came to the door.

"Piper. The name's Piper. How do you do, madam?" He responded.

"I'm doing quite well, thank you for asking. That's an interesting look you have there, Piper," she said to him.

"Well, I am a Jed—" He said before I interrupted.

"Mom, we're on a tight schedule. We have to go. I'll be back around ten," I said as I saw Piper lick his fingertips and then rub his rattail with them. "I mean, seven."

I led Piper to my garage to get my bike and felt him rub my ass again as I opened the garage door.

"Listen, you'd better fucking stop with that, I'm serious. You were doing it yesterday when we were looking for my cousin. You pull that shit again and I'll punch you in the face. I'm not joking," I said.

"What are you talking about? I adhere by the highest virtues. I would never, ever do such a thing," he responded.

"Then how do you know what I'm referring to?"

"Pretty cool garage," he said, changing the subject.

I ignored him and grabbed my bike. This was the first time I was hanging out with someone who I think was around my age in a long time. He was actually a pretty cool guy at first. He was doing some neat tricks on his bike. I have to say that I was impressed. As we were passing Horace and Ninth, we saw a comic book store that was opening up.

"That's pretty cool, right?" I said, looking at the comic book store.

"Yeah, I guess. Comics are pretty lame. I bet they sell swords and run a sweat shop in there," he said.

"What would make you say such a thing?"

"Look at them – they're Asian,"

"That's a terrible thing to say, weirdo."

"I'll make you pay for calling me that," he said in a serious tone.

"Huh? I was joking, Piper. But, that Asian thing you said was pretty offensive."

"Oh? I get it. Yeah, that was pretty funny," he said.

I noticed that he still had my phone number written on his forearm. He had drawn a heart around it. He saw that I noticed it, so he started pedaling ahead of me.

He peddled as fast as he could, leaving me behind, and made a U-turn. As he was quickly peddling back to me, he let go of his bicycle handle, stretched out his arms, and started singing, "*I feel so alive/for the very first time/and I think I can fly…*"

"That was P.O.D.," he said. "They're a rockin' band."

"Oh?"

"I like to sing that as I ride fast. It's pretty bitchin'."

"I bet," I said.

"You should try to sing that while you peddle pretty fast. It'll make you feel *alive*," he said with a smirk on his face.

"No, I think I'd rather not," I responded.

We reached the mall without saying much after that P.O.D. moment, which I find embarrassing even as I write this. The mall was packed, as usual.

"It's packed here," I said.

"Yeah. It'll just take some kid standing there with a hard-on sticking out of his pants. Hope I don't go breakin' it off," Piper said.

"What? What are you talking about?"

"Oh, I just quoted *The Crush*. You know, the movie with Alicia Silverstone?"

"Oh, I don't know what to say about that, Piper, I honestly don't."

What were the odds of Piper and I running into Sally Marshall at the mall? I thought they were pretty slim, too, until I remembered that Sally was a teenage girl and probably spent more time at the mall than at her house.

"Hi, Alexpiss," she said to me. She was with two other girls.

"Good to see you, too, Sally," I said.

"I see you're here with a boy!" She said.

"Hi, my name's Piper," he said as he put his hand out for Sally to shake.

"Piper? Alexpiss, you're dating a guy named Piper? How, like, dumb is that?" She said and laughed with her friends.

"Sally is your name, huh?" Piper said. "You have such pretty blond hair," he said as he pet her hair.

"Ew, get away from me, freak," she said as she and her friends quickly walked away, totally – and rightfully – creeped out. "Have fun making chimp fetuses," she said. It was pretty gross and ironic, considering she'd probably even suck a gorilla's dick if she had the chance to.

Anyway, petting Sally's hair was an ultra-weird gesture, but I liked the fact that he made her uncomfortable. It's too bad he also made me feel the same way.

"She was pretty cool," he said.

"She's anything but. Hey, there's the arcade I was talking about. Want to play?"

"Sure, I guess…"

The arcade was really cool. It had foosball, ping-pong, air hockey, the works, on top of a ton of arcade games. I'm sure you've been there. You could verify how cool the arcade mall is without me having to write about it. It was also where I first played *Street Fighter 2.*

"You know, I've never actually played this game before," I said.

"Me neither."

"Play with me."

"Alright."

For a kid who was literally every sense of the word 'geek,' Piper sucked at video games. I kicked his ass so badly that it was pretty boring. It was probably more fun pretending to play the demo to see how the game is played than it was actually playing with him. We went on to play air hockey, and he sucked at that, too. He had no sense of real fun at all. He looked like he was having a miserable time.

"Are you having any fun here, Piper?" I asked him after an hour.

"No, not really."

"What do you do for fun?"

"I do stuff, I don't know."

I was curious as to what a self-proclaimed Jedi does for fun. I wanted to explore Piper's world.

"You don't know? Why don't you take me to a place where you have the most fun?"

"Really?" He asked in disbelief.

"Sure, why not?" I said surprisingly.

He led me out of the mall. We got on our bikes and rode eight blocks. We stopped in front of a house.

"This is where I live. Want to come in?" He asked.

I was pretty nervous to go inside his house. I was also kind of pissed because I had dug this hole for myself. I was going to be on my guard the whole time in there, and was ready to punch him in the face at any cost, despite the fact he has an insane mother.

"Sure, I guess I'll follow you in, Piper," I said to him. "But, I'll only step inside if I walk behind you."

The interior of his house was unreal. Everything had plastic covers over it – even the refrigerator. There were holes cut out around the door so it could be opened and closed. There was a big chalkboard in the middle of the kitchen. I was so freaked out and curious as to why this kid and his family were weirdos.

He took me to his room, and it looked like the way you'd expect. He had pictures of different spaceships from various television shows and movies, a huge *X-Files* poster with his head pasted on Agent Fox Mulder's body, and a picture of an alien that had the caption 'Abduct Me!' under it among other things, like a sealed box that had 'DO NOT OPEN UNTIL 2025…SERIOUSLY!' written on its side.

"We'll be off to Never Neverland in two seconds, baby. Let me put this on," he said as he pulled out a CD and inserted it into his stereo. "Make yourself comfortable on my bed."

I saw a white spot on his pillowcase, which I'm still pretty sure was dried semen. His walls have probably seen things no man or pubescent boy should ever see.

"I think I'll lie on the floor," I said as I lied down.

"Wise choice," he said. I still don't know why he said that.

He turned the lights off, but the room was still illuminated with the glow-in-the-dark stars he had all over his ceiling. He put Metallica on the stereo. I'm not sure which song it was, but it sucked – it all sucked. To make matters worse, he turned on a fog machine that was next to his dresser. The generator's hum battled with the Metallica song charging out of the speakers. Eventually, his room was filled with fog.

He laid down next to me and started playing air drums while headbanging.

"Listen to this part…Oh, yeah, you hear Lars hit that? It is unreal! It is unreal!"

I quickly grew bored, but was afraid to storm out because I knew he'd have a conniption. I continued lying on the floor and tried not to fall asleep. I figured that I'd never be the same again if I would have fallen asleep because I was fairly certain things that should never be inside of me would have somehow ended up in there, knowing this freak. I didn't trust him or his greasy, sweaty hands one bit.

After about three minutes, I heard banging on the wall. It scared the shit out of me, while making Piper lose his. He got up and started banging back on it.

"NO! NOT THIS TIME, MOM! I FINISHED ALL OF MY HOMEWORK! THIS IS *MY* TIME! DON'T RUIN IT! YOU RUIN EVERYTHING! THIS IS MY TIME, FUN TIME! YOU SAID, YOU SAID!" Piper screamed as he then proceeded to kick the wall. I remained silent and looked at my watch. It was five-sixteen. He lied back down on the floor next to me after his fit.

"You know," he said to me in a calm and soothing voice. "I'm glad we're spending this time together. I don't know what I ever did without you. We share a common bond. You're my little Padme. I'm your Anakin, and I would kill myself if you ever broke up with me," and then he kissed me on the cheek.

A chill went so fast and far up my spine that my scalp went numb. I started to envision starving children in Ethiopia, polar bears tearing baby seals' heads off of their bodies, human eyes being gouged out of their sockets, and stuff of that nature.

"That's it, I'm out of here. I can't take this anymore. I really can't. Piper, you're one fucked up kid in the fucking head. You really need to see a psychologist to get it fixed! You may have left it in a galaxy far, far away or some shit—"

"Yeah! A Star Wars reference! I like where this is—"

"Shut the fuck up! I fucking hate Star Wars! I hate your house, I hate your music, I hate the fact that I'm here! I'm so out of here! If you follow me, I'll pepper spray you and your mother!"

"Does this mean you're not going to the next Star Wars convention with me?"

"Piper, leave me the fuck alone. I don't know you, and you don't know me from this point on. You have serious issues. I *will* file a restraining order against you if you come near me again. My parents are divorce lawyers!" I said as if they were *real* lawyers.

I heard the banging on the wall again.

"Yeah, fuck you, too!" I yelled out to his mother and stormed out. I heard Piper throw a fit in his room. He started knocking stuff off the shelves. I then heard his mother storm into his room.

"PIPER, WHAT THE FUCK IS GOING ON HERE?" She screamed. She had a hoarse voice. I heard glass shatter, and after I heard that, I sprinted the fuck out of that house and rode my bike back like I was competing in the Tour de France. I was faster than lightening. I had never felt such a surge of adrenaline.

When I got home, I ran into my room and was grateful to know my parents were assholes and not psychopaths, like Piper and his mother. I got chills knowing that somewhere, he had a father.

I accepted the fact that I was going to be a different breed of loser for the rest of my life. There are many sects of loserdom. I decided from that point to be a loner loser; someone who would rather play Connect Four by herself or something like that. I'll wait until college to meet new friends. High school was a lost cause. I didn't really try to hang out with anyone else again, and still don't.

My parents are still retarded, as usual. I think both of them are actually having affairs, but that's a whole different can of worms I'd rather not write about. That's the reason why I'm in detention, anyway. It's fucked up to ever say anything about a dysfunctional family to someone who's in it. That's what Sally did.

"So, Alexis, I saw your mother pull out a beer in the beverage isle at the supermarket and start drinking it while coked up or something. It was kind of funny to see her dragged out of there while screaming about citizens' rights or some crap like that. I think your daddy was also getting a handjob by a client of his in his car at that same supermarket's parking lot. Whoops!" She said.

I was, both, relieved and offended. I was relieved because she had stopped calling me 'Alexpiss.' It's not that it bothered me in the first place. It's just that it was a weak insult. I mean, if you're going to use something, make it good, and not corny. I was offended by the other thing she said, though. It wasn't her place to air out my family's dirty laundry. I would slit this slut's throat for my parents' honor, even though they're both very far from perfect. It also made me pissed because it was most likely true. I'm still pissed as I write this. Who the fuck was this bitch to say shit? Seriously! What gave her the fucking right? So, I did what anyone else would have. I laughed it off and waited for her to turn her back to me. When she did, I pulled her by the hair, smashed her head against a locker, and started wailing away at her face. I'm in detention and could face the repercussion of not walking at my graduation ceremony, but I don't care. I'm still going to go away to college. And besides, I don't have any friends here to cherish the milestone with.

Anyway, I recently heard news about Piper. I should have written this a few lines up to have some sort of flow here. I got caught up in the whole 'I'm alone in this world and I've accepted it' angst bullshit, but better late than never. I saw him one afternoon a couple of months ago as I rode my bike past the comic book store. He still had the rattail. I'm lucky that he didn't see me. My cousin, being in that geek subculture, said that Piper's now some prodigy in *Street Fighter 2*. Go figure, right? According to my cousin, the kid went ape shit after I stormed out of his room, and went through this whole transformation. I heard that he now went by the name AsSaSsiN – with alternating capital and lowercase letters. He said that the name Piper no longer pertained to him. He said that Piper died a tragic death, and that he would take on a new being and find a new calling in video games – particularly *Street Fighter 2* because it was the only game the comic book store by his house had. It's a good thing that Piper didn't see what my cousin looked like under the ewok costume he had on when they met because I'm sure he would've kidnapped him for ransom or something. I know he must have watched me while I wasn't aware in the past few months. It's so creepy to know he knows where I live and has my phone number. I'm still weary when I hear my phone ring only once.

So, anyway, it's almost time for me to leave. Thanks for reading if you've read this far. I changed my mind, and am not going to kill you. This venting actually made me feel a little better. As you could tell from the beginning of this entry, I felt like shit. Please don't think I'm sappy, a bitch, or a loser. My parents suck, the guy who's ever shown a serious interest me is a creep, and I don't have any friends because no one understands me or I don't understand them. There. The explanations are packaged in a neat sentence right there. I'm going to hide this in a secure place where I know it will take a complete accident to find, and maybe years. I can't believe I've written as much as I have.

Well, reader, this is the end. Mr. Bryan said we have about three minutes left, and to start packing up. You'll never know if you ever ran into me because I'm outta this school in a few weeks. How weird is that? That's the way things always ought to be. Everyone should get to know a stranger this way. It would make life much more interesting. Goodbye, reader, and may you have a better high school experience than I did.

Take care and don't stare at the sun, stupid.

   - Alexis

## THE RISE & FALL OF THE RAISINETTES

"You didn't clean your room, Stuart?"

"No, grandpa, and I'm not going to do it. I ain't gonna live by rules and responsibility. Chaos sells and I'm buying."

"What the hell are you talking about, Stuart? You're only twelve years old."

"Grandpa, it's just that I'm tired of this Capitalist society enforced by rules. It's not what I want to invest my life in. It's not how I roll on my Razor scooter, you know what I mean?"

"Stuart, you march into your room and clean it, now!"

"You ain't the mother of me, ain't the father of me, you ain't nothing of me. The only thing you're doing is endangering my lungs by filling it with your old man dust."

"That's it, get over here. I should have told you this a long time ago. It's a story I heard about not too long ago. It's not a nice story that's filled with pumpkins and guitar-playing butterflies. Just shut up, sit on my lap, and I'll tell it to you."

"You've wanted to tell me a story you heard not too long ago since a long time ago? That makes no sense. I'll listen to your stupid story, but I ain't sitting on your lap."

"Since when don't kids sit on their grandfathers' lap for a life-altering story?"

"Since like the fifties. It's a weird thing to do, dude. I dare you to tell me otherwise."

"Fine, sit on the couch, and I'll tell you the story of the most rumble and tumble gang any town has ever seen. This story will teach you what will happen to you if you continue to foster that attitude of yours for long. It starts off with a teenager named Daniel. Stuart, stop smelling the couch cushion after you've farted on it and listen to my story, damn it. It's rude and disgusting!"

"Ugh, grandpa! Fine, tell me your retarded story for retards."

Daniel was a fourteen-year-old who was neglected the attention he desired from his parents. He was often overshadowed by his younger brother, Toby. Toby was eleven years old. He always wore fitness outfits – headband, sweatpants, etc. – and would constantly attempt to impress his mother while they were at the supermarket, at the bus stop, in the subway, wherever, with his endurance. In this particular instance, they were in a subway car.

"Hey, mom, want me to do fifty push-ups here? I'll do it. Fitness always equals first place," Toby said as he dropped to the floor to do fifty-one push-ups. He always did one extra than he said he would do and dedicate it to his mother.

"Forty-nine, fifty, and this one's for you, mom. Fifty-one. Free of charge…"

"That's my little Jack LaLane! You're so strong! You're my little Kevin Costner as my bodyguard. Daniel, why don't you try to get more in shape like your little brother?" Their mother said.

"Mom, stop comparing me to Toby! For the last time, I really hope you'd stop! Look at him and look at me! I am not Toby. I will never be Toby!" Daniel said while Toby was doing pull-ups on the handlebar.

"Well, no, you'll never be like Toby – especially by poisoning yourself with those candy bars. Look at your reflection in the window. You look disgusting," his mother said.

Daniel looked at his reflection and saw his mouth covered in chocolate. He was addicted to chocolate, and didn't care how he looked as he ate it – much to his mother's chagrin.

"I will no longer be giving you your weekly allowance. The money goes to waste. It goes towards those candy bars. You're cut off, Daniel."

"Aww, but mom! It's not fair!"

"Life's not fair, big bro," Toby said as he did his twenty-third pull-up.

Daniel thought this was an injustice. He didn't want to go on without having his cherished chocolate. Now that he couldn't fulfill his chocolate lust, Daniel would walk past the local hangout spot for soon-to-be misfits, Mr. Pippens' Chocolate Utopian Nougat Town, and sulk as he looked through the front window at all the chocolate he would now have to miss out on because he had no money to buy any. All of this happened because he was a pig. He did this for two weeks until he couldn't take the duress anymore.

One Friday afternoon after school, Daniel went into Mr. Pippens' Chocolate Utopian Nougat Town and did something unprecedented in his life. He grabbed handfuls of Whatchamacallit candy bars and stuffed them in his pencil pocket – yes, the pocket in the schoolbag where he stored his sharpened pencils. He liked the mechanical ones where you click from the top to make the lead come out from the bottom. He didn't like the regular wooden ones because they would break easily. He always had to make sure they were No. 2 because his geometry teacher, Mrs. Fitzsimmons, had a propensity for surprise tests, and so he always wanted to have a No. 2 pencil in case there was a Scantron test and couldn't use any other pencils. Oh, my, I've gone off into a tangent. I'm so sorry, Stuart. Where was I? Oh, yes, he stuffed his stolen candy into the pencil pocket of his schoolbag, quickly walked out of the candy store, and turned the corner into the alleyway. There, he slumped himself behind a dumpster and got his sugar high like a heroin junkie dejected by everything in the world except for the syringe he's injecting into his veins. Daniel was in a delirious state of hedonism and gluttony. It was a disgusting sight. Remember, he didn't have a care in the world for how he looked whenever he ate his chocolate – especially when he hadn't had a taste in weeks. It was a ravenous scene.

Something terrible happened after that. He grew accustomed to stealing, and thus began an evil common practice. Every other Friday for two months, Daniel would go into the candy store and extort approximately twenty dollars worth of candy. Mr. Pippens' store didn't have any surveillance cameras or security guards. Mr. Pippens, himself, would have never foreseen someone committing such a heinous act in his store. His hat would have flown off of his head if he had any inkling!

Daniel would go into the candy store while it was packed with kids wanting their chocolate fix. He would morph into someone else whenever he got into his new criminal mental state. His pupils would dilate, and he'd be the personification of evil and greed. Daniel had a malevolent look on his face whenever he'd go into Mr. Pippens' store to steal. He was addicted to his candy, and it would take months – possibly years – of chocolate detoxification to cure him of his sugary needs.

One particular Friday after two months of stealing candy, he noticed someone in the store wearing a black hooded sweatshirt glancing at him numerous times. Daniel felt threatened by him and kept his distance. The intimidation could have stemmed from the fact that this particular person had ripped jeans and fingerless gloves on – you know, the kind of gloves that Bender character had in that popular 80s high school movie you made me watch, *The Breakfast Crew*, or something like that.

Daniel grabbed a handful of candy and ran out of the store. He feared attracting any attention, but was disconcerted by the black-hooded stranger. He ran into the alleyway, next to the dumpster where he'd eat his stolen chocolate, like an addict who'd commit deplorable sexual acts to members of the same sex for just one snort of cocaine. He stood petrified for three minutes until he heard footsteps coming closer to him. He had a bad feeling about everything and regretted stealing candy in the first place. The sound of footsteps ceased. Daniel let out a sigh of relief – until he heard a wrapper being opened. He heard the footsteps nearing again. Daniel almost excreted a brick bigger than your dog Rocky dropped after you gave him those Thanksgiving leftovers. Remember that? You gagged for about three days. Anyway, it crossed Daniel's mind to make a run for it. Then, the black-hooded stranger turned the corner of the dumpster and stood face-to-face with Daniel.

Stuart, from this point on, I must warn you that the rest of this story will have filthy language because, you must remember, these were street urchins. They were up to no good, and their vocabulary was just as ugly as they were.

"Howdy, partner," said the stranger.

"Uh, hi," Daniel said.

"I've been watching you for days."

"Oh? I've never noticed you."

"It must be because I just bought all these new clothes. I thought I needed a fashion readjustment. I got a raise on my allowance, and – no, wait, shut up."

"What do you want?" Daniel asked nervously.

"I know what you do. I'm on to you," the stranger said as he winked and scratched his genitals.

"What do you mean?"

"I like your style. Innocuous and yet a motherfucker."

"Excuse me?"

"I have a filthy mouth. So sue me. My dad's a lawyer anyway. I noticed your pattern from day one. You come in every other Friday. Every day, though, you stare from the outside in and plan your attack. I saw you put that candy in your book bag."

"What do you want? Leave me alone!"

"Oh, frisky. I like frisk. You remind me of a kitten."

"What?"

"Nothing, man, I'm all sorts of crazy! I'm the craziest motherfucker to ever fuck mothers. You may have seen my tag everywhere. The name's Wise."

"Wise? Oh, yeah, I've seen that tag. You always tag in bathroom stalls, right?"

"Guilty as charged! I don't give a fuck if I ever get caught. And if you bust me, your bathroom wall is next, fucker. I'm a crazy son of a bitch."

"You really are extreme, man."

"Let me tune you in to a little secret, dude," Wise said as he came in closer to Daniel's ear and whispered, "I'm supposed to be studying for a big exam right now. I told my mom I was going to the library. Guess where the fuck I am right now."

"Where?"

"Um, I'm in this alleyway talking to you right now."

"Oh, yeah, that's badass, man."

"Dude, I...don't...give...a...fuck..."

"Wise, you're just about the toughest guy I've ever spoken to. My name's Daniel, by the way."

"Hey, Daniel. You ever talk to a crazy motherfucker before?"

"No, this is my first time, and I must say it's exhilarating."

"I'm the craziest they come. I don't give a fuck about nothing," Wise said, apparently also 'not giving a fuck' about grammar, Stuart.

Daniel, startled by Wise's demeanor, was becoming more nervous.

"Wanna see how much I don't give a fuck, Daniel? I'm gonna take a shit right next to this dumpster. I DON'T GIVE A FUCK!" Wise proceeded to unbutton his pants and crouched next to the dumpster.

"YOOO! Wise, you're so crazy, bro! You don't give a fuck about nothing! Don't take a shit by that dumpster!" A voice Daniel didn't recognize said. It came from another person walking into the alleyway holding a bag of groceries. Daniel considered running away.

"If it isn't my tag-teaming, double penetration partner," Wise said as he stood up and buttoned his pants. "Daniel, this guy and I have gotten our dicks stuck in more holes together than a gopher." That was not true at all, and couldn't be further from the truth.

The person who came into the alleyway wore the tightest pants any guy should ever be allowed to wear. He had slicked-back hair, a white shirt under a leather jacket, and a red bandana in the back pocket of his jeans. It was the so-called rockabilly look, Stuart.

"Daniel, this is my boy, Veto. Veto, this is my baby brother, Daniel."

"'Sup?" Veto said.

"Hi," Daniel responded.

"How you doing, bro?" Wise asked Veto.

"Ok. Just got some groceries and was heading home to get my dirty laundry when I saw you here about to take a shit next to this dumpster."

"Shit, you know how I do, Veto. Yo, Daniel, this guy's almost as crazy as I am. Whenever you pass a pre-school's playground, don't be surprised to find his name on one of the jungle gym bars. He don't give a fuck like me."

Daniel wondered why he was called Veto. He always wondered from that point until Wise told him three seconds after he first wondered why.

"Wanna know why we call this fucker Veto?"

"Sure," Daniel said.

"Well, this hard dick always vetoes any idea you have. For instance...Hey, Veto, I want to go to the diner and get some milkshakes. Sound good?"

"No," Veto said.

"You fuck, you got me again!" Wise said. Veto shrugged his shoulders.

"Anyway, I must be going, guys," Daniel said.

"Not so fast, Daniel. After observing you for a few weeks, I got a splendid idea for an organization, and I thought you might want to be in on it. You know, the candy here is easier to steal from than my grandmother's purse. She has dementia and cataracts. Anyway, we could steal this candy and sell to the kiddie market. Kids would suck dick for candy – especially chocolate. That's a big market to get into. I'm talking huge. What do you say we steal this candy and sell it to them for some profit?" Wise said.

"I don't know. Kids don't have a lot of money, and besides, how in the world are we going to sell to them without looking suspicious? Also, we're in school. We don't have time to sell to them during recess," Daniel said.

"We have someone on the inside who'll sell to them, and he'll feed us our profit. The only thing is that we have to get stock to the middleman. We'll keep a stringent inventory to make sure the little prick doesn't steal from us," Wise said. "We'll need someone like you with your catlike candy-pickin' skills to steal them from Mr. Pippins' place. I didn't call you kitten before just because you're adorable. For school dances and shit like that, we could infiltrate the schoolyard and make a killing on those nights."

"No," Veto said. Wise ignored him because he understood it was in Veto's nature to disagree with him.

"It'll just be us? The three of us? It sounds too big of an operation for just three people," Daniel said.

"We've got it all covered. You'll be joined by a few people. We've got friends, bro, friends," Wise said. "All we gotta do is just be careful TMB don't get any word of this."

"Who?"

"It doesn't matter. Are you in or out? We could sure use you. I ain't messing around. Look at Veto. He wouldn't mind having you as a member of our team," Wise said. Veto stood with his head turned looking at people walk past the alleyway, oblivious and apathetic to the conversation.

"Will I get anything out of this?" Daniel asked.

"Sure you will. You'll make ten percent of what we rake in. We won't get caught. I even made up a name for us to coincide with this operation. It's so ill."

"Well, alright, I suppose I'm in. I wouldn't mind making some money and eating all the chocolate my little tummy could handle," Daniel said.

"All right! Daniel, you won't regret this. You will make so much money, eat so much candy, and finger so much pussy," Wise said.

"Really?" Daniel and Veto said in synchronicity.

"Well, no, we don't really get girls, but we'll certainly build up enough street cred that it could be feasible...one day..." Wise said. "So, I say bring on the pussy."

"Yeah, bring it on. I wouldn't mind smearing some of that on my face," Daniel said.

"Look at this motherfucker. He's already fucking shit up. I like him. Daniel, welcome to The Raisinettes. We're the craziest motherfuckers this town has ever seen. Yo, I don't give a fuck, I'll take a for real shit right here," Wise said and unbuttoned his pants again.

"Yo, Wise! Not again! Bro, you're so crazy! Don't do it, bro, don't do it!" Veto said. He appeared to only speak whenever Wise was threatening to defecate in an alleyway.

"Alright, this time I won't, but who knows what my capricious mind will decide to do later on? I really need a straitjacket for Christmas. You got a cell phone, Daniel?"

"Yeah, you want my number?"

"Yeah, give it up, bro."

That set a new standard in Daniel's life. When he got home, he ran to his room and changed his instant messenger profile. In the 'occupation' section, he changed 'pain in the ass' to 'candy dealer.' He felt accepted, and adopted a new attitude. The phrase 'I don't give a fuck about nothing' kept reverberating in his head. His new attitude manifested itself at the dinner table that night.

"I could eat these Brussels sprouts in three and a half minutes, then do twenty jumping jacks, and then twenty sit-ups. It will all be done in seven minutes. Want to time me, Daniel?" Toby asked.

"Toby, I don't give a poop," Daniel responded.

"DANIEL THEODORE MONROE! WHAT DID YOU JUST SAY?" His mother screamed.

"Nothing, mother, I said nothing."

"That's what I thought."

"Yes, that is also what I thought, boy," his father added.

"See, Stuart, it was starting to get pretty bad."

"Grandpa, this guy Daniel is a pussy, and his friends are even bigger pussies. That Veto guy and that other guy are the biggest tools. Grandpa, I'm bored by this story. This is worse than the one you told me about that kid whose hand had a mind of its own after he masturbated, and it ended up strangling both of his parents while they slept. I'm not buying it. When does this story get more action?"

"Oh, you want action? Why didn't you say so? I would have skipped all of this introductory stuff and gotten right into the gang without having to explain Daniel's backstory. I'll skip over a lot of the stuff between now to when The Raisinettes started their operation."

There was a cast of characters in The Raisinettes. First off, of course, there were Daniel, Wise, and Veto. As far as the others, there was Fungus, Tiny Jim, Piper, Mothman, Snotfuck, Ponytail, Keanu, and Reeves. Fungus was the only member with an ironic name. He had obsessive-compulsive disorder. He always wore gloves, and would enter and leave a room three times. Wise thought himself a literary scholar, and thought no one else knew that he named Jim 'Tiny Jim' after Tiny Tim from Charles Dickens' *A Christmas Carol*. Snotfuck was a scary one. He had a tattoo. It was a tattoo of Yoda, but it was scary, nonetheless, because he was the only one in the bunch with a tattoo and a bad attitude. He was also the only one in The Raisinettes who smoked cigarettes. He would buy a pack, take one puff of a cigarette, and then flick it. He never took more than one puff of a cigarette, but still, he was scary. Wise's little brother, Brian, was the middleman, and an unofficial member – even though Wise told him he was an official one. The gang would meet at their secret location – the basement of Wise's house, in Brentwood Estates. It was a closed, tight-knit community that was tough because it had tall trees and its own community patrol. It was to haul out miscreants – and despite what others say, it was not because it's a gated, chic high-income community.

"Alright, dorks, here's what we need to work on," Wise said. "We need to—"

"Elijah, would your play buddies like to join us for dinner?" Wise's mother yelled downstairs.

"MOM! For the last time, it's Wise! Please respect that! And, my GANG MEMBERS would not like any dinner!"

Veto, of course, disapproved and shook his head.

"Whatever you say, hon," Wise's mother said.

"What the fuck, Wise?" Reeves protested.

"Dude, shut up, what did I say about language here?" Wise said.

"But, I'm hungry!" Reeves exclaimed.

"Then go home and suck a fart out of your mommy's ass," Wise retorted.

"Good one, Wise," Brian said. Brian looked up to his brother and the other gang members. He was honored to be in the same room as them. He thought they were the coolest bunch of guys. Wise was never impressed.

"Yawn. Anyway, Brian made about twenty dollars in candy revenue," Wise said. "That means we're all getting a piece of this honey pie, and it tastes so sweet."

"Yes! All right! Awesome! Radical! Too cool! Totally Tubular! This is most satisfactory, indeed!" Various members of the gang said.

"Alright, shut up! Listen up, girl scouts—"

"Yeah, Wise, way to rag on the guys," Brian said.

"Go to your room, Brian. Get out of here," Wise said.

"But, Wise…"

"Go upstairs now, Brian, or you're out of the gang."

"But—"

"Don't make me say it again. Please don't make me say it again. You know what, scratch what I said. I want you to make me say it again. Please, I'm begging you, ask me to say it again because I want to show you what will happen," Wise said.

Brian didn't say a word. He hung his head and walked up the stairs. Yes, Stuart, in case you were wondering, he *did* close the door behind him. Good boys do that. You should try it sometime.

Wise continued, "Now where was I? Oh, yes, Jefferson Junior

High will have its sock-hop dance this weekend. I propose that we show up with a bucket of candy and make some sales. I don't want a throng of people showing up, though. We don't want to attract any unnecessary attention. I propose I go with Daniel, Snotluck, Fungus, and Veto." Wise never said Snotfuck's name properly while at his house because he didn't want to get in trouble.

"Oh, fuck you, I ain't going," Veto said.

"Veto, please, when we're outside of my house, you know that I don't care what sort of language you use or how crazy you are, but while we're in here, we have to keep it cool, alright?"

"Whatever," Veto said.

"Alright, so here's the deal. Daniel, you think you could get us some candy by Friday? The dance starts at eight o'clock. We could swing by at like six-thirty, scout the place, and divert any people who could thwart our moneymaking. I guess it'll just be four of us," Wise said.

"What about the rest of us?" Mothman inquired.

"Mothman, I guess you'll have to do something else that night. I mean, we could rock this town another time, and you'll be a part of that crew. For this candy operation, though, we're going to have to keep it low," Wise said. "So, Daniel, will you be able to get us a buttload of candy on Friday?"

"Yeah, I guess so. I'll need someone with me to cause a diversion."

"Snotluck, you're going to have to go in on this one, what do you say?"

"Whatevz," Snotfuck said as he glared at the Yoda tattoo on his forearm.

"Alright, so it's settled. Now, guys, sorry to be so abrupt, but it's Wednesday and I've got a lot of homework I need to finish up. Raisinettes out," Wise said. "No, seriously, get out. I have to finish my English paper. Ponytail, do you need to call your parents to come pick you up? Anyone else need to use my phone?"

"Grandpa, I'm still waiting for the action. You just told me about a corny geekathon orgy in some kid's basement. Where's the good stuff?"

"I'm getting to it. I had to tell you what led to the school sale."

"You could have just gone straight to that instead of telling me about this."

Anyway, it was Friday afternoon, and Daniel and Snotfuck went into Mr. Pippens' Chocolate Utopian Nougat Town to steal the stash for the dance. Snotfuck was to be the diversion while Daniel stole the candy. Snotfuck approached the cashier and brought forth his best diversion tactic.

"Hey, dude, I see you have a Pandora's Box shirt. Those guys rock. You into Magic Cards? Remember when they were pretty cool to play? Just kidding! They're still cool to play! You in?"

"I can't right now, dude. I'm working," said the cashier.

"Alright, cool. So, how old are you? You look like you're over forty. Why are you working here? Is this where you've always wanted to work? You married? Probably not. Tell me, man, what gives?" Snotfuck asked.

The cashier looked at Snotfuck and got teary-eyed.

"Nah, man, you think I thought I'd be working at this fucking place all my life? It all started back in the summer of '79..." and then he went on with his story.

With the diversion working, Daniel had the clearance to have free rein with the candy. He stole Milk Duds, Hershey bars, Rolos, Chocolate Koala bars, M&M's, etc. His schoolbag was packed, and he looked conspicuous holding it. He ran out of the store. Snotfuck was intrigued by the cashier's story and stayed.

While running out, looking back, and not paying attention ahead of him, Daniel ran into a man wearing overalls and worker boots sucking on a pacifier.

"You betta' watch out where you be runnin', niño," the man said. "You don't know who I am. I could cut your balls off, drink the blood, and leave you for my dogs to eat, yes-sir, mm-hmm, I ain't jokin'."

Daniel ran the other direction while the man glared at him with a piercing look. When Daniel passed the candy store again, he crashed directly into Snotfuck as he was coming out of it, causing the both of them to fall on the pavement. It was slapstick at its greatest, Stuart.

"What the fuck!" Snotfuck yelled.

"Sorry, I'm really sorry. We gotta get out of here!"

"Nah, it's cool, man, that guy has his guard down. I could set this place on fire, he wouldn't care."

"No, you don't understand, I think I ran into some maniac. He threatened to drink the blood out of my balls…"

"Your ball-blood? Oh, shit, what did he look like?"

"He was wearing overalls and had a pacifier."

"Fuck! Come on, get up, let's go. Quickly. Let's get out of here. I have to get in touch with Wise."

"Are we running away from this guy?" Daniel asked as they were both quickly walking away.

"Come here, let's go into this backyard," Snotfuck said as they walked down a residential block.

They went into a random backyard and hid. Snotfuck, obviously distressed, pulled out a cigarette, took one puff, and flicked it.

"You obviously know who that guy is," Daniel said.

"That guy is a member of The Mamma's Boys," Snotfuck said.

"Who are they?"

"They're our rival gang. We don't get along. We just can't. The guy who you ran into was Raul. He always threatens to drink the blood from your balls. It's his motif. The Mamma's Boys wear overalls and suck on pacifiers. We tear shit up while they suck on pacifiers. Their queen is hot, though. Anyway, we can't let them know what we're up to. We own this market, and if they get in on it, it'll start a gang war. Do you want a gang war, Daniel? You want the shit to hit the fucking fan and splatter on your front doorstep? Just think about what your mother will say. She'll probably call all of our mothers. That would just be abominable. Because once there's a war between The Raisinettes and The Mamma's Boys, all shit is going to hit that fucking fan. I need another cigarette."

"You're hooked!"

"Don't you think I already know that? I know I'm a chain smoker. It's an early grave for me, man, an early grave. It'll be an even earlier one if we cross paths with those Mamma's Boys," Snotfuck said as he flicked the cigarette. "Come on, we have to meet up at Wise's house and get ready for the school dance." They started walking again.

"I thought the name 'The Raisinettes' was made up specifically for this operation," Daniel said.

"No, Daniel, we've been a gang for just over a year. The Mamma's Boys and us haven't gotten along since day one. We formed and started walking around our turf in a big group, all of us – and then ran into The Mamma's Boys. They called Wise a 'used tampon,' sprayed us with water guns, and all hell broke loose. It was the beginning of March! The weather was still cold! Tiny Jim got sick! We just don't get along. It's like cobras and polar bears. They'll never get along. No matter how man tries to get them to live harmoniously, they will never be able to coexist in the same ecosystem. You catch my drift, Daniel? I'm wising you up, novice."

"Yeah, Snotfuck, I read you loud and clear."

That night was a night to roll out the punches and leave the bullshit at the bus stop. I'm sorry to be so crass, Stuart. Daniel, Wise, Snotfuck, and Fungus got to the school to begin their latest operation via bus. Fungus had to exit and enter the bus three times when they boarded and un-boarded.

Once they got to the schoolyard, Wise sent Daniel and Fungus to scout the area.

"You think those Mamma's Boys will be here?" Daniel asked Fungus.

"Mamma's Boys here? When? Where? What are you talking about? For real?" Fungus inquired.

"No, I'm just asking you."

"Oh, shit. Are you trying to give me an ulcer? You know about my disorder, right? Everyone's always fucking with me. One of these days, people will regret fucking with Fungus. You'll personally be on that list of people, Daniel. You'll really find out who's *really* fucked up once I finally get rolling with my plan."

"I wasn't messing around with you, Fungus." Daniel thought it would be best to not talk to Fungus anymore.

Upon further inspection, the coast was clear, and the selling was able to commence. The problem was that they were two hours early. No one was showing up for a while. Wise thought it would be great practice for being covert. They hid in the bushes in front of the school. After two hours of silence and not saying a word, Phillip showed up. He was one of the biggest buyers. Wise popped out of his hiding spot.

"Howdy, cowboy," Wise said.

Phillip was younger than the four candy dealers. He feared them solely because of their age.

"H-h-hi, Wise. What brings you here?" Phillip asked.

"Let's just say that daddy's gonna get paid tonight," Fungus said.

"Fungus, what did I say about you talking during deals? What did

I say?" Wise asked.

"Sorry, Wise, I thought it would be fitting. I've been wanting to use that line—"

"I don't fucking care! Just shut the fuck up. Here," Wise said as he picked up a worm from the grass and threw it at him.

"FUCK! FUCK! WHAT THE FUCK!" Fungus screamed. Daniel grabbed it and threw it another direction. Fungus looked at him and said, "You know this doesn't change shit. You're still on my list."

Phillip was terrified.

"Just ignore him, Phillip," Wise said. "I got some primo shit here, dude. You wanna take a peek?"

"Uh, sure. You got any gummy worms?" Phillip asked.

"Gummy worms? Are you a dyslexic five-year-old? No, man, I don't have that kind of shit. Do I look Puerto Rican to you? I said primo shit. I have chocolate, Phillip, chocolate. Daniel, get over here with the bag of chocolate. You scared, Phillip?"

"Yeah – I mean, no – why?" Phillip said.

"Just asking. Do I make you nervous, Phillip? Are you afraid of me?"

Phillip began to shake.

"N-no, Mr. Wise, I'm not afraid."

"Good, as long as we're friends. If I'm cool, then you're cool. Am I right?"

"Yes, Mr. Wise, one hundred percent."

"Daniel, where the fuck is the bag? You know any other guys who'd like to get into this fresh shipment of Tootsie Rolls, Phillip?"

"They're not Godiva chocolates?"

"Godiva? Do I look like a pussy to you? If you take off my pants, you'll find an anaconda dick. And it ain't afraid to expose itself to a girl. Want me to prove it? Get me a girl's digits and I'll call her. I don't give a fuck, Phillip, I'm crazy like that. We don't eat or deal that pussy Godiva shit. Seriously, though, do you know any girls, and could I get their numbers?"

"No, Wise, I don't."

"It's cool, it's cool. I got three girls I'm fucking anyway. I'm kind of busy and don't need more of that at the moment." Nothing about that sentence was true.

"Yeah, I bet," Phillip said. Daniel showed up with the bag Wise requested.

"Here's the candy I have," Daniel said as he opened up his schoolbag.

"Easy pickins, some good lickins," Wise said to Phillip. He would have flipped a lid if anyone else had said it.

"I like this stuff. I'll take three Tootsie Rolls and four Hershey Kisses," Phillip said.

"My man likes the expensive shit. I like your style. You rollin' with the Benjamins tonight?" Wise said. "That'll be a buck-fifty."

"A dollar-fifty? That's a rip-off! That's more expensive than what your brother charges."

"I ain't my brother. Yo, don't make me scratch your mother's car. I know where you live, and I don't give a fuck about nothing," Wise said. "I'll even ring your doorbell at two in the morning on a weekday and run the fuck away, motherfucker."

"I just think this price is unfair," Phillip said.

Snotfuck grew frustrated with Phillip for being a cheapskate. He walked up to him, pulled out a cigarette, lit it, took one puff, flicked it, and sternly said, "Just pay us the buck-fifty, kid. You don't want to mess with street punks like us."

"Alright, alright, but—" Phillip said before footsteps were heard around the corner. Wise put his hand over Phillip's mouth and pulled him into the bushes.

"You fuck... You wearing a wire?" Wise whispered to him.

"What?" Phillip asked.

"I said, are you wearing a fucking wire?"

"No!"

"Were you followed? Did you tip off a chaperone? If you did, I will egg your fucking house. Look into my eyes. Look at them. I ain't joking. You know what I don't give, Phillip. Tell me what I don't give. Whisper it into my ear."

"A fuck?" Philip whispered.

"Correcto-chango, Tango and Cash, Phillip. You hit the jackpot."

"I didn't tell anyone anything! I swear it! Please let me go. I lost my sugar tooth. I just want to go to the dance. I swear I won't say anything."

"Shut up, someone's coming!" Snotfuck said.

It turned out to be three girls attending the dance. One of them was in a wheelchair, the other had orthopedic headgear on, and the third had a cast on her left arm. The latter two were skipping next to the girl in the wheelchair and singing, *Que Será*. They soon entered the gymnasium.

"That was a close one!" Fungus exclaimed.

"I want to go home. I don't even want to go to the dance anymore. I just want to go home!" Phillip said. "There's a party at Mickey Henderson's house tonight. You guys should go there and make a ton of sales."

That captured Wise's attention.

"I'll crash his party with my boys. We're that hardcore. I'll do it by myself, I don't care. Daniel, call up the rest of the crew and tell them to come. Where does this douchebag live, Phillip?"

"I'll tell you, but please let me go!"

"Fine, then go home, cry-baby. Go cry to mommy and suck on her toenails, loser. You're such a nerd. Um, could you give us the address now, please?" Wise said. "Boys, let's skip this joint and make some real money."

The boys left Phillip sobbing in the bushes and went off to their new destination, Mickey Henderson's house, on 1627 Maple Lane, one block east of McKinley Park.

The whole gang all met at McKinley Park and marched to Mickey Henderson's.

They heard music blasting from the inside the house. Neither of them wanted to ring the doorbell and ask to be admitted inside.

"I think you should do it, Wise," Mothman said.

"No, man, I don't want to. You know I always tear shit down to the ground, but I don't feel like it right now. How about you, Daniel?" Wise said.

"No way. I have the candy," Daniel responded.

"Um, fine, how about Veto?" Wise asked.

"Bad idea," Veto said.

"You motherfucker, you got me again!" Wise exclaimed.

Veto shrugged his shoulders.

"Fine, then, how about Snotfuck?" Wise asked.

"I have a better idea. How about we wait for someone to walk out the front door, and then we rush inside?" Snotfuck said.

"Alright, we'll have to go with that," Wise said.

It took about twenty-five minutes, but someone eventually came out of the house to throw up on the front lawn. This almost made Fungus go into cardiac arrest.

"Now's our chance to get in!" Wise said, and they all ran inside the house through the open front door. It wasn't as cool an entrance as they had hoped because Fungus had enter and exit through the doorway three times. What they found next was something that would be controversial for years to come. It appears that Mickey Henderson was in cahoots with The Mamma's Boys. Yes, Stuart, the same rival gang that The Raisinettes were afraid of. Huddled around the couch next to the front entrance was a crew of fifteen grown men dressed in overalls and sucking on pacifiers. Now, did Phillip intentionally and maliciously send them to an ambush? That question has never been answered.

"Well, well, well, if it isn't Dee Raisinettes," Raul said. "How are you doing, Tiny Jim? Not coughing or having a case of how you call dee sniffles?"

"No, I'm just fine, thank you very much," Tiny Jim said.

"What the *fuck* are you little pussies doing here?" Hernando asked.

"We came here for a party, Hernando, what else, dude?" Wise said.

"Hey, guys, looks like the party has gotten pussies for all of us to fuck and not call in the morning," Hernando said.

"Yeah, and it stinks!" Marty, a member of the Mama's Boys, said.

Hernando was visibly upset by Marty's comment.

"Marty, you're lucky we have an affirmative action clause in the gang charter, or else your white ass would have been beaten down ages ago, wey," Raul said. "Mammi, mammi, where are you, mammi. We need you. Wah, wah…"

Out from the kitchen came the most attractive Asian woman any of The Raisinettes had ever seen. She was slender, had emerald-colored eyes, soft skin, silky dark hair, and wore a dominatrix outfit. Her name was Yvette, and she was The Mamma's Boys' queen.

"Oh, poor baby, did these nerds give you a buzzkill?" She asked.

"Goo-goo-ga-ga, mammi. I wuv you, mammi," Raul said.

I forgot to mention to you, Stuart, that The Mamma's Boys always spoke to Yvette in baby talk. She was their queen and surrogate mother.

"Baby, you need burping?" Yvette asked.

"Not now, mammi, but maybe later, after these pussies are slapped around," Raul said.

"What the fuck are you nerds doing here, anyway? Aren't you

supposed to be sneaking a peek at one of your sister's tits?" Yvette asked.

"We're tired of you guys always messing with us. We want it to end right now. We came here with other intentions, but while we have you guys here, we want to send you assholes a message. The Raisinettes will *not* tolerate any drive-by water balloons tossed at us or being pelted with vegetables you find on the street. Just think about what it does to Fungus here. We're sick of it, and I frankly don't think this town is big enough for the two of us," Wise said.

"What are you trying to say, Raisins?" Yvette asked.

"First off, it's The Raisinettes. Second, what I'm saying is gang war," Wise said, bringing an immediate hush over the room. Fungus nearly fainted, but had second thoughts when he realized the floor was very likely dirty. Mickey Henderson was nowhere to be found.

"Dis motherfuck want a gang war, this motherfuck get one," Raul said. "I will get drunk on his ball blood."

"Raisinettes, you think you've really got it in you to face my baby boys?" Yvette asked.

"Cock-a-doodle-doo, I just said that. I don't want to mess up Mickey's house with the roughhousing, though. Where is he, anyway?" Wise said.

"He said he was going to get some chips, but never came back. Men, go figure…" Yvette said.

"Yes, I suppose you're right," Wise said. "Looks like we can't have this gang fight after all," Wise said.

"Wait a second. We could do it at McKinley Park! That's like a block away from here. Mammi, could we do it there? Please, mammi? Mammi, please? May we kick their asses at McKinley Park? Pretty please?" Hernando asked.

"Baby, mammi will see what she could do. How's that sound, Raisinettes? You want to unleash a hellish fury tonight at McKinley Park?"

Wise thought it over. He was tired of being made fun of, tired of being the butt of pranks by these Mamma's Boys. He wanted to finally be accepted as a legitimate baller. He made the agreement.

"Yes, that sounds good," he said.

Daniel looked at him and whispered, "Wise, what are you getting us into?"

Reeves whispered, "I'm scared, Wise. I'm about two breaths away from dropping a deuce in my Alf boxers."

"Could you Mamma's Boys excuse us for a second? I need to talk to my crew," Wise said.

"Yeah, you could blow each other in the kitchen. It's right over there," Yvette pointed and said.

"We'll be right back. Raisinettes, assemble!" Wise said. "And we will *not* be blowing each other while we're in there!"

Once in the kitchen, Wise gave his momentous gang leader speech.

"Raisinettes, I, as your fearless leader, will never, ever put you in danger that would not merit glory. We could finally end the year of torment we've suffered from these assholes. Remember when we tried to have that Super Mario Brothers-themed party? They showed up and egged us. Remember when we had that sleepover in Ponytail's tree house? They showed up and egged us while we slept. I'm sick and tired of that! I can't stand it anymore! I will no longer tolerate it! Us walking in to The Mamma's Boys is serendipitous. I can't see a better way to end this perpetual bullshit than through a gang war. If we fight, we will look upon ourselves this evening as heroes, and not like candy pushers who were given a bad tip and weren't able to make even five dollars for the night. No, I'm tired of this bullshit. Tonight, each of you guys will be somebody. You just have to believe in yourselves. We're the fucking Raisinettes, the leanest and meanest motherfuckers this town has ever seen. We've got Fungus. He'll cough on you, for real, he don't give a fuck. We've got Veto who will verbally shoot your shit down. We've also got Ponytail, and we've also got everyone else. I'm a crazy motherfucker, and under my wing, I will not allow you to lose and tarnish your name or the name 'The Raisinettes'! We could vindicate ourselves tonight. I *will* take a shit in the kitchen sink, I don't give a fuck!"

"Yo, Wise, don't do it, bro, you're mad crazy!" Veto said.

"Yeah, Wise, please don't take a shit in Mickey's sink. You are mad crazy, fearless leader, and I will follow you anywhere," Tiny Jim said in a somber tone.

"Yeah, me, too," "I'm in." "As long as you're there, Wise, I'll go," various members said, and everyone agreed to follow him. The Raisinettes stuck together for the cause of defending their name. They took a stand for once, and would not sit back down this time. They walked out of the kitchen and accepted the challenge.

"We accept!" Wise said.

"Well, I'll be damned. Alright, Raisinettes, you're on. I guess we'll meet you at McKinley Park in a half-hour. I need to change some of my boys' diapers," Yvette said.

The Raisinettes walked to McKinley Park and waited for half an hour. They were nervous about the outcome. Wise gave them reassurances.

"We'll be ok," he said to them.

The Mamma's Boys walked into the park. Yvette had an ultimatum.

"My children and I have discussed this. We thought that it would be best that whoever lost would have to disband."

Wise agreed to the condition.

"I have faith in myself and my boys," Wise said. "You're on. Loser must disband their gang. If you guys win, The Raisinettes will never be heard from again. The same goes for you, right?"

"Yeah, that's part of the deal. I proposed it," Yvette said.

"Welcome to the dance. Let's rock," Fungus said.

Wise angrily looked at Fungus and said, "Fungus, I want to have a word with you after the fight. So, anyway, how do we do this? An all-out brawl? Melee? I have so many questions."

"Well, I guess it'll be an all-out brawl, so come on, hit Raul," Yvette said.

"No, Raul, you hit me," Wise said, looking at Raul.

"No, hit me," Raul said to him. Everyone else circled one another, unsure who should throw the first punch. It was then Raul who did it, but missed Wise and accidentally hit Fungus in back of the head. Fungus fell to the ground faster than a hooker with a broken high-heel who doesn't pay her pimp on time – or so I've been told. That prompted Hernando, Marty, and the other Mamma's Boys to throw punches, and The Raisinettes found themselves on the ground in the fetal position as The Mamma's Boys kicked each one of them.

Wise finally screamed out, "Alright, enough! This is an unfair advantage! It's a slaughter! We give up, we give up!"

With Wise conceding, Yvette told her gang to stop pummeling The Raisinettes. The Mamma's Boys felt sorry for them.

"So, it's settled, you pussies are to disband immediately. You could no longer use the name 'The Raisinettes' ever again, and we'd better never see you guys walking around together," Yvette said.

"We're not allowed to hang out with each other at all?" Daniel inquired.

"No, on second thought, that's too harsh. Fine, you could hang out, but you can't ever use the name 'The Raisinettes' again. That name is defunct. Also, you can't tag up anymore. Your tags are officially dead. You cowards didn't even put up a fight. I saw how my beautiful babies kicked each one of your asses." Yvette said as she and her Mamma's Boys walked away.

Hernando took Daniel's schoolbag full of chocolate. The now-defunct Raisinettes stood together in the dark park defeated. The silence was disrupted by Fungus' sobbing. Each former Raisinette was disgusted with himself. They collectively realized they were not nearly as tough and rugged as they thought they were. As they walked out of the park, they noticed a car driving towards them with its headlights off. When the car approached them, they saw Raul stick his head out of the back passenger seat. He pulled out a semi-automatic gun.

As the car slowed down, Raul yelled, "Rest in peace, motherfuckers," and began to shoot.

The boys who used to be The Raisinettes dropped to the ground to dodge the bullets. Raul could be heard laughing maniacally as the car then peeled off.

"OH, SHIT!" Wise yelled. "This isn't a fucking joke! Is everyone ok?"

"Are you guys alright?" Someone asked.

"I want to go home!" Someone said.

Everything was a blur. A loud shriek came from the park. It was Snotfuck. He yelled for help. When the boys caught up to him, they saw he was holding Tiny Jim on the ground. He had blue paint all over his chest. Raul had shot at them with a paintball gun.

"No! Not Tiny Jim!" Wise yelled. "Tiny Jim, are you ok? Answer me! I need to know! Fuck! Answer me!" Tiny Jim didn't respond. He began to cough, but did not respond verbally.

Wise continued, "We gotta get him to an emergency room! Hang in there, Tiny Jim! I don't know what I'd ever do without you! Hang in there! We'll get there soon, just hang on! He has allergies! Someone help me take him to the hospital! He has allergies!"

"I'm not going to tell you whether Tiny Jim lived or died. It doesn't matter. I hope you learned your lesson, Stuart."

"Grandpa, that was a waste of time. What did you possibly think I would learn from that long and drawn-out story?"

"That even though you think you're the toughest kid on the block, there's always someone tougher than you."

"If there is any moral, it wouldn't be that. It would be that if some pussy who thinks he's tough isn't really tough, then he's still a pussy."

"No, I liked my explanation better, Stuart."

"Grandpa, don't you suffer from those episodes?"

"They only come up sporadically."

"Whatever, grandpa. If there's anything that story did, it's pique my interest in smoking pot. You just wasted so much of my young life with that incredibly lame story. I'm so outta here."

## ONE IN THE PINK, EIGHT IN THE STINK

Have you ever committed a crime? Come on, you can tell me. I won't tell a soul, I promise. I'll admit to some devious slips in inhibitions. After all, I'm only human. I will admit something to you as long as you come clean about the dirtiest, most illicit act you've ever committed. Between only you and me – and the other people who read this – I once took a puff out of a marijuana cigarette when I was seven years old. My older brother's friend said I would be able to fly like Batman if I did. I should have realized two things at the time before I took the puff – or as cooler kids these days call it, a 'hit.' First off, I had seen numerous after school specials that dealt with the subject matter of taking a puff – or again, a 'hit' – of marijuana. It made kids stupid. After smoking it, they'd have premarital sex, have a baby they didn't really want, and would then resent it. The baby would then grow up to be a homosexual or a rapist – whichever came first. The second thing I should have realized was that Batman does not fly. Anyhow, I took a puff out of the cigarette and inhaled it as my brother's friend had instructed. I then got an unusual warmth that resonated throughout my body like a smoky haze through a dark alleyway infested by crack whores giving birth to crack babies, pimps slapping their hoes across the face because they didn't meet their monetary quota, and thirteen year old boys in a masturbating competition. I saw and heard nothing but images of Peter Falk making farm animal noises across each room. I was so afraid that I jumped out of the second story window of my house. It's a shame I went through the garage roof, face-first. I was a pothead. I smoked a tree, I saw Mary Jane, I shot a hook shot, I shot a load, I slammed a fat girl, I did whatever it is kids these days use as slang to refer to smoking marijuana. I did it all. I was a junkie for that one puff. That's why I became a cop – and if you admitted to smoking a marijuana cigarette or answered the first question I asked with an affirmative, then put your hands up, motherfucker, you're under arrest.

My name is Lieutenant McKenzie Cooper. I spearheaded the war on drugs in Monroe County for three years. I created a special law enforcement team devoted to taking down drug kingpins, drug lords, drug kings, drug tyrants, drug dictators, and drug emperors. My unit's team was called The Maulesters. We bit and mauled the drug dealers who were polluting our streets. Most boys on the force would look up to us. They respected what we did and how we handled things, and I welcomed it.

"You're such a child molester, Lieutenant Cooper," Michaels said once.

"Thank you, son, just doing my job," I responded. "But, I think you mean drug maulester."

"Right..." Michaels said, acknowledging his mishap.

Our unit was under somewhat of a lull, as there were no reported incidents of drugs in over two years in Monroe County – a moderately quiet town with an occasional hiccup or two of crime. There was once a loud party that didn't let down until two in the morning. I know what you thought as you read that last sentence: 'Ever hear of a little thing known as 'sleep'?' I know, but that's not even the worst of it. There was once a guy at the party who was going to turn twenty one years old two days from then, and had taken a sip out of a beer can, the police report read. I wanted to put that punk in jail for thirty days, but the judge wouldn't allow it. He's too soft on these kids. We haven't gotten along since.

I was relocated to six districts in ten years. Monroe was the quietest out of all of them. When I worked out in the city, I saw things no man should ever see – let alone a sexy lady. For instance, I once answered a call to some poor schmuck who jumped out of his office window. After he had landed and left a mess of guts, blood, and organs on the pavement, some Albert Einstein wannabe took a piss on the corpse before the cops showed up. We arrived to see his pants pulled down to his kneecaps while a stream of piss and blood flowed between the toes of his bare feet. Sorry to paint a gruesome picture, but I wanted to convey the rawness of the types of things I saw as a cop. Being a cop in the city was not limited to depressing stories dealing with urine, blood, semen, hair, Guatemalan babies, and feces. I also witnessed acts of love, such as an adorable act of adulation when a coked-up junkie punctured her forearm with needle marks that spelled out the name of her boyfriend 'Harvey.' I'm surprised she wasn't dead considering how much heroin intake she consumed. It's stuff that like that still makes me a sap. We didn't get incidents like that here. However, as far as I'm concerned, that sort of thing could be left in the city. Let us good folk stay in peace. I'm not saying that everyone here is an angel or a do-gooder.

I once had to answer a call concerning some son of a bitch who was backyard wrestling with his friend while his parents were out of town. Roughhousing for a kid is a harbinger for having a heroin needle in your arm while drooling blood from your mouth and ass by the time you're sixteen years old. It's a serious gateway crime. Anyway, while searching his house, we found that this nerd had these movie posters all over his bedroom walls of movies like *Harry and the Hendersons*, *Howard the Duck*, *Stop! Or My Mom Will Shoot*, *Mac and Me*, *Cop and a Half*, you get the picture. And get this, in his closet, I found some pirated DVD's.

"Hey, Steven Spielberg," I said to him. "Mind explaining these to me?"

"I-I-I…" He said. I didn't know what he was saying. I was starting to suspect he was under the influence of drugs. I handcuffed him and his friend.

The both of them wanted to know what it was like to be wrestlers, right? I backhanded the host so hard that his mother would have been proud of me. I pity her, though, because that's something *she* should have done long ago. I wish I could have slapped her so hard across the face while she was pregnant with him, that he'd have felt it and had thoughts about strangling himself with the umbilical cord before committing any heinous act like the one I busted him for. It's not my job to 'parent the parent' as I say, but I'll do it with pleasure anyway. I like to consider it as working overtime.

The kids here needed to be put in their place. It was my badge that gave me the authority to be a hard-ass, a tight-ass, a tough dick, a big dick, and whatever terms or phrases kids these days use to describe people who enjoy doing their jobs meticulously like I do. I welcome it because I know I'm good at what I do. Also, what's with kids these days? I often wondered what the matter with kids was these days while I sat at my desk listening to the CB. I still wonder about that. Maybe it's the fact that I have too much time on my hands these days, or maybe it's because my wife of thirteen years left me recently. I just don't know why I still think about what the matter is with kids these days so much either. I think I should really see a psychiatrist. That's another story that has yet to be published – so, don't bother looking for it at your local library.

Once while on patrol, I ran into a couple of skateboarding kids hanging out on a stoop.

"You kids sure are up to nothing," I said as I stopped next to them.

"We're just hanging out here on my stoop, officer. How's your evening going?" One of them asked.

"That is not any of your concern, son. What are you kids up to?"

"N-n-nothing, officer. Why do you ask?"

"Just let me stick with the questions, Cedric the Entertainer," I said, throwing in a pop culture reference I knew these kids would understand, which allowed me to connect with them more. "I see that you have a shirt that reads 'Minor Threat.' Are you trying to tell me something, punk?"

"That's just the name of a band, officer."

"Do bands take any time to think of names these days? Flock of Seagulls was the last good band name to ever be taken. Has music after the early eighties really depleted that much?"

"Actually, officer, they were around in the early eighties," one of the kids said, referring to the band on his shirt.

"You trying to be smart with me, smart guy? I should pull your pants down, lay you across my lap, and spank your bare ass until your mother gets a headache."

"No, officer, I wasn't trying to be smart."

"Just wanted to get that straight, son. Anyway, why don't you kids listen to nice music?"

"We do."

"Oh, really? Well, what other music do you listen to?"

"Well, we're into all types of music. I recently downloaded a leaked Ricky Rocket radio session."

"Ricky Rocket? Downloaded? Leaked? I don't read you, son."

"I have an album by the musician Ricky Rocket that was recorded at WXBK a while ago. It was leaked, meaning it hasn't been officially released, but someone posted the files on the internet, so I downloaded them."

"That legal? Isn't that infringing copyright laws?"

"I think it's legal, as long as it's not widely distributed, I believe."

"You believe?"

"Yeah, I'm pretty sure."

"Ricky Rocket. Now, why does that name sound familiar?"

"Don't know, officer. Maybe because his music made people kill themselves by jumping out of buildings and walking into traffic?"

"Made people jump off buildings and walk into traffic? Is that what it takes to be a positive role model among kids these days?"

"I don't know."

"You kids should listen to nice music. Ever hear Howlin' Howard & The Mamma's Boys?"

"No, sir, I can't say that I have."

"You should certainly pick up their album. That's nice, wholesome music I could get silly to while listening. They have this amazing fiddle player who – wait a second, is that an image of a marijuana leaf on the deck of your skateboard? You guys intend on smoking a marijuana, aren't you?"

"Shit, Jeremiah, let's get out of here!" The other kid sitting next to the kid I was talking to said.

"Run!" The kid I was talking to said, and he and his friend scattered.

I was livid.

"Oh, you fucking punks, that's it! I'm going to knock your fucking teeth out as I shove this baton down your throats," I said as I chased after the son of a bitch who was ostensibly named Jeremiah.

It was the most action I had experienced in years, and it was a good thing I worked out every day, knowing this day would eventually come. I was certain this no-good-mother punk wouldn't get away. I was prepared to fill out any paperwork about the 'accidental' pistol-whip I was going to give him. I chased him through Main Street. He whizzed past pedestrians walking down the street enjoying their day and zigzagged from one side of the street to the other. He looked behind to see if I was coming, not noticing the two kids coming out of Mr. Pippins' Chocolate Utopian Nougat Town. He slammed right into one of them, causing himself and the other kid to fall onto the ground, spilling the innocent bystander's Goobers and Milk Duds on the sidewalk. I halted and grabbed Jeremiah by his hair.

"Are you civilians alright?" I asked the kids who accidentally got tangled in Jeremiah's web. "Just know that you've aided the Monroe Police Department in apprehending this fleeing suspect. Thank you. I'm sorry for the loss of your candy."

"Not, not, not a problem, officer," one of the civilians said.

"What's your name, son?" I asked.

"Henry," he said.

"Well, Henry, you're the kid cop of the day. You're going to be a top ace someday. I love you for that, I really do. Now, if you'll excuse me, I have empty out the douche," I said as I pulled Jeremiah's hair.

I had some good old-fashioned police brutality fun with our dear friend Jeremiah, which I can't get into now. All that you should know is that he had three marijuanas in his pocket and that I made sure he'll have to piss with one leg lifted in the air like a dog for the rest of his life. Nope, he won't be forgetting the name McKenzie Cooper anytime soon.

I was starting to lose my grip with reality soon afterwards. That incident got my adrenaline pumping faster than a jackrabbit mating with a crippled squirrel. I started to workout to the hardcore folk sounds of James Taylor. I was craving more action, but there was nothing going on in the streets of Monroe. Oh, that was until I came across a couple that had stuffed the body of a kid they hit in the trunk of their car. What dicks, right? That was around the same time we discovered a couple of bodies stabbed in the throat at Monroe Park. What the fuck was this world coming to? Stabbed in the throat. Go figure, right? I thought I was going to have to give an evil motherfucker a prostate exam with the long arm of the law up his ass once we found him. The only eyewitness was of no use to us. He was some unreliable sap who gave a less than useful description. There were no real leads. All of a sudden, murders started springing faster and harder than an Asian kid throughout our small town of Monroe, but mostly centered in or around the park. It seems as if this little serial killer thought it was funny to stab civilians in the throat with no apparent motives. We kept getting the same eyewitness for these murders – which was way too much of a coincidence. We were starting to suspect that he was the guy reporters dubbed as 'the Monroe Murderer' until we found him stabbed in the throat and handcuffed to his stove. I guess it was our mistake that we didn't guard him as well as we could or should have, but it's alright because he didn't have a wife or children. He was perhaps a hormonal homosexual, so that's one less sordid individual polluting our streets. I have my own theory about those types of people. I'll save that information for the children's book I'm planning to publish. Anyway, things were too hot to handle and too cold to hold with those murders. So, as I said, nothing really going on in the streets of Monroe these days.

Before his "unfortunate mishap" while in my care, Jeremiah told me about his marijuana drug dealer who transferred to Monroe High from Middleton in order to infiltrate the Monroe market – a hotbed for losers, deviants, and asshole kids looking to score some shit. He was little Timmy Johnston, a tenth grader with a bad attitude and an even worse math sense. Even though I was in my mid-forties, I petitioned the chief to allow me to spearhead an undercover sting at the school as a student in order to catch little Timmy in what I thought would be a relatively easy bust. I'd soon discover he was elusive.

I dressed the part of a teenager for my undercover operation by I shaving my beard and to look like I was sixteen and not forty-six years old. I parted my hair down the middle of my scalp, and had to stop getting my biweekly crew cut from my barber Jarvis. I had to tell him that it was nothing personal when he noticed I didn't come in the second Thursday of the month. He was so worried that he dialed

911 when I didn't show. I also tried to take up skateboarding. When that didn't pan out as well as I had hoped, I decided to not actually ride one, but to hold one and always threaten to skate away from school if a teacher was giving me the third degree. I also purchased an electric guitar, homemade Ricky Rocket t-shirts, army fatigues, and those Chuck Taylor Converse All-Star sneakers I see youngsters wear. I've heard them labeled as 'indie.'

I had consent from the principal of Monroe High to conduct my operation without any faculty hindrance. My undercover name was a clever one. I switched my first and last names. My undercover self was Cooper McKenzie, sixteen years old, originally from Bergen. Why'd Cooper McKenzie – or shall I say Coop – move to Monroe? Don't you worry, Silly Sally, I did my homework to answer that one, so just sit quietly on the living room couch until daddy comes home. Well, the 'official' reason would be that my parents got divorced, so I lived with my dad. I'd mention that my dad was on the run from the cops for drugs. That would allow me to blend in more and build street cred with little Timmy. It's called feeding the mind of the perpetrator. I believe the official police terminology for it is 'lying.' I needed to prove to my classmates that I was as badass as they were, and that I also disregarded the rules. Cooper McKenzie was no mamma's boy.

I was enrolled in Timmy's English class. I eavesdropped on the kids trickling into the classroom and heard that the teacher was a tight-ass. He sounded like someone I could admire. I thought maybe he and I would share some sort of kinship.

"Alright, take your seats, everyone," Mr. Plimpton said as he walked into the room. "I have word that we have a new student here by the name of Cooper McKenzie. Welcome, Cooper. We're currently in the middle of reading and analyzing both of Homer's epics, the *Iliad* and *Odyssey*. Did you cover Homer at your previous school?"

"Nope," I said sounding like a jaded teenager.

"Oh, well, are you at least familiar with Homer?"

"Nah."

"Oh, that poses a potential problem. I'll try to work with you as much as I can so you're up to speed with the rest of the class."

"Oh."

"I see you're not much of a talker. You know, some of the

124

brightest minds in history were not social butterflies – similar to the way you're currently demonstrating."

"So?"

"I see you're not only bright, but also clever by answering with another monosyllabic word."

"Huh?"

"That's the spirit, Cooper! I see that you're going to be a valuable asset to this classroom! You're making a great first impression. Now, class…" He continued.

I had no idea what the fuck he was talking about. Homer? I was starting to suspect drugs. He most likely got them from little Timmy. That son of a bitch had already beaten me to the battlefield so quickly in the game!

"Fucking brain," some kid to my left whispered to me while scratching himself underneath his desk.

I raised my hand to backhand him across his fat, pimply face, but realized I didn't have a badge to protect my rights, so I had to put it down.

When class let out, I went to my locker to get books for my next one. While there, I was approached by Timmy, himself, and the goon who sat next to me in class, whom presumably had the sweat from his balls on his fingertips after he had scratched them repeatedly throughout class.

"Hey, brain," Timmy said. "You're the new kid in Plimpton's class."

"Yeah," I said not seeming interested. I was playing it real cool.

"Allow me to introduce myself. The name's Timmy. This here is my right-hand man, Davy."

"Gimme one," Davy said as he extended his hand out for me to slap. I was apprehensive of touching it. I was afraid my skin would melt off if I did.

"Nope, think I'd rather not," I said.

"Meow," Davy said.

"Shit, that's fucked up. Not gonna give my boy some skin?" Timmy said.

"I have a germ phobia," I said thinking on my feet.

"Whatever, man," Davy said as he picked at his teeth.

"Yeah, whatever is right. My name's Cooper, but my bros, dudes, and two aunts call me Coop. And I've got a bad attitude," I said.

"That's pretty badass, Coop," Timmy said. "Anyway, I thought I'd introduce myself and let you know I'm here for whatever you need – if you know what I mean," he said as he winked at me – giving me either a gay insinuation for oral sex or to clue me in on his marijuana dealings. I was uncertain, so I tried to kill two birds with one stone. I lowered the zipper of my jeans and then mimed smoking a joint with my fingers.

"Why'd you unzip your pants?" Timmy asked, and that's when I knew he meant the marijuana, and not oral sex.

"Oh, I just thought I'd get the breeze in," I said.

"That's a pretty good idea. I sometimes get some air clutter in there, too," Davy said.

"Anyway," Timmy said. "Yeah, if you want to take a high flight, if you know what I mean, pass me a note in class. I'm always carrying some of the green stuff."

"What kind of green stuff you talking about?" I said wanting him to implicate himself.

"You know, the good stuff."

"You got any right now?" I asked while leaning forward from my open locker, thinking I could bust him right then and there.

He hit his forehead with his open palm as if he forgot something.

"You know what? I don't right now. I know I said I did, but I don't at the moment. I misspoke, I guess. Hey, I gotta go. Come on, Davy," he said and quickly walked away.

He was acting very suspicious, and I had to get to the bottom of it. I turned towards my open locker and realized it wasn't a good idea to hang pictures of myself with fellow Maulestors and my police badge. The son of bitch eluded! He was better than I gave him credit for. That's when I knew high school kids aren't as stupid as when I was a little boy. I needed to up my game.

When I got home, I was so furious that I worked out harder than I ever did before. I took my frustration out on my pectorals. They took a beating that night, but I rewarded my body with a protein shake – banana flavored. That night rocked as far as that, but sucked as far as school. I needed to regain Timmy's more-open-than-necessary trust towards someone he just met.

I ran into him in the hallway before first period the following day.

"Hey, boyfriend, you totally left me whet with wanting some primo pot. Ram it in me, holmes," I said, speaking in slang kids use today.

"I'm not gay, dude, and you're a narc. I was just playing around yesterday when I said that stuff to you," he said.

"Me, a narc? You're kidding, right? Hey, if you're referring to that badge and picture of me with cops, you've been fooled by Coop. That's me! I'm Coop!"

"Explain, then."

"Well, my dad's a cop. He's a real big, hard juicy dick full of cum, you know?"

"Yeah."

"Yeah, so anyway, I like to bust his balls and rim his job by taking his badge every so often. You should see him looking for it," I said. I leaned in close to him and whispered, "One of these days, I'm gonna take his fucking gun and shoot a stray dog with it."

"Oh, shit! You'd better call me when you do that shit, seriously!" Timmy said credulously. "Then, explain the picture with the cops…"

"That was last Halloween. That was my Halloween costume with some of my bros."

"Yeah, makes perfect sense! I was dumb to think you were a narc, Coop. You're a badass iguana and shit. You know what I mean, right?"

I then started doing my best iguana impression, but I instead began to walk like a duck in circles while licking my lips.

"Yeah, man, like that! A fucking iguana and shit! You're badass," he said.

"Yeah, well, I've gotta get to class," I said. I was hoping he'd invite me to have lunch with him and his cronies so I could have an in with them.

"Hey, Coop, why don't you cut and join me with some of my buds?"

That was an even better idea.

"Yeah, why not? Fuck this place. I've been aching to skateboard the fuck out of here since I got here yesterday," I said as I pointed to my skateboard.

"I wouldn't go that far, dude. This is a good institution for kids like us. Each year, the federal and local government cut more and more school funding. Look at our fucking classrooms! How productive is a teacher going to be with one computer for every five students, outdated text books, and classrooms where kids have to fucking stand up due to lack of space?" He said as he got teary-eyed. "What you said is totally fucked up. An education is the greatest tool, asset, necessity, whatever to overcome oppression, and is mightier than any gun, bomb, or missile."

"Sorry, I guess you have a point," I said as I realized he was cutting class and not heeding to his own spiel.

"Come on, let's get out of this fucking place," he said, and we walked out of school. We met up with seven of his goons at the park adjacent to the building.

"Hey, wet dicks, I have a new homie here who wants to hang with us. His name's Coop. He's new around these parts, so treat him with cuddles, alright?" Timmy said. "Coop, this is my crew. This is Davy. You remember him from yesterday, right?"

"Yeah, 'sup?" I said to him.

"Meow," he responded.

"That's fucked up, Davy, he's one of us, dude," Timmy said.

"Why does he meow?" I asked.

"That's his corny-ass way of calling you a pussy – you know, like a pussy cat."

I wanted to slap that filthy-mouthed son of a bitch across his fucking teeth. He had some nerve to meow at me in that context. Timmy continued to introduce me to the other guys.

"This here is Dwayne. He's a master at water polo. He will make you suck his dick in the game, that's how good he is. I get hard-ons watching him in action. He's so good. He'll pawn your ass, motherfucker. He's also really into Cat Fancy, and is a totally weird dude. I don't think you guys should interact with each other, actually," Timmy said as we walked past him.

We then came across a kid who was standing next to the trash can looking like he was going to throw up. He reeked.

"This here is Dirty Dick Daryl. This guy fucks so many girls in so many zip *and* DVD regional codes! He likes to keep the scent of every girl he fools around with on him, so he never washes his genitals. That's why we call him Dirty Dick Daryl. His name isn't even Daryl – it's Earl – but we couldn't think of any other names that started with a D," Timmy said.

"But, there's David, Dan, Damon, Dennis, Daniel, Dylan, Diego, Douglas, Dominic, Dean, Dexter, Donovan, Drew, Donald, Desmond, Duncan, Danny, Darren, Dario, Demetri, Denzel, Dilbert

– and you even have two guys here named Davy and Dwayne—" I said before I was cut off.

"Yup, no other D names…" Timmy said.

"Hey, Dirty Dick," I said.

"What's up, dude? What's your name?" Dirty Dick Daryl responded.

"Coop."

"Hey, Coop. Hey, you got any Cheetos on you?"

"Alright, Dirty Dick Daryl, that's enough out of you," Timmy said and pulled me away by my arm.

"You know what," he said. "These guys are fucking weirdos. I don't think the other four guys are even worth introducing you to. If you thought Davy, Dwayne, and Dirty Dick Daryl are out of their minds, then Dale, Dante, Derek, and Dustin might as well be fucking aliens. You don't have to meet them. Listen, I don't have any stuff on me right now. But, I could get you some by tomorrow if you're interested. I'm the only dealer in town, so you know I'm gonna have the goods then."

"Sure, yeah, that's cool. I'll just pick some shit up tomorrow and get higher than John Lithgow," I said.

"That's what I'm talking about! Hey, you listen to Death Kills In Millions?"

"DKIM? No, can't say I've ever heard of them," I said.

"Oh, alright, well, I start singing some of their lyrics to pump me up," Timmy said and started singing, *"Get out the way, motherfucker/ cuz don't you know that I'm on the prowl, kid snatcher/ You're gonna see me commit lyrical genocide/ and then you'll start to gawk/ I'll proceed to look at you and say/ 'See ya at Pizza Hut, motherfucker, with Tony Hawk.'"*

"Those are cool lyrics," I said.

"Yeah, I'll send you an MP3 sometime. Hey, what are you doing tonight?"

"Nothing, why?"

"All of us are gonna see *Taco Bell: THE MOVIE*. Wanna come see it?"

"I don't know, it's rated R. Aren't we too young?" I said testing him.

"Fuck that! It's the hottest movie in town. We're gonna get tickets for *A Rainbow For Harriett* and totally sneak the fuck into the movie, and watch the shit out of it!"

I began to realize that these fucking brats are the reason why this country is going to shit. They abuse the system, they abuse the Motion Picture Association of America, and they abuse movie theaters around the world – from Afghanistan to Zimbabwe. It was clear that these animals held nothing sacred.

"Yeah, I'm in," I said. "I hear the movie rocks the house." In actuality, even though the movie had shattered box office record after box office record around the world, I didn't have even half an ounce of interest in it.

"Cool, dude, it's gonna rock harder than EVERYTHING ZEN, EVERYTHING ZEN! I don't think so!" Davy said, even though he wasn't part of the conversation.

"Yeah, Bush still totally rocks! I don't care what anyone says, their music isn't dated at all," Timmy said as he played air guitar. "Wanna go after school, Coop?"

"Like I always say, 'let's go,'" I said.

"That's a cool motto. It makes you seem like you're always ready and willing to go," Timmy said.

I knew I had an in with the crew now. I was ready to make my move at the theater and then bust the son of a bitch and his goons the following day. I first needed to swoon them some more. The rest of the morning with these schmucks was as eventful as drooling on your own dick for three hours. I don't really care to go into details.

After school, I met up with the gang at Timmy's locker. Timmy was in the middle of a story when I caught up with them.

"So, I was like I'll sell you a dime bag for two-thirds the price. Guess what. The dumb fuck gives me half instead! He totally gave me more money because one half is more than two-thirds," he said. It was at that point I knew that he was getting ripped off by each of his clients.

"Hey, bros and dudes, when are we gonna hit up the tacos?" I said while rubbing my stomach, referring to watching *Taco Bell: THE MOVIE*.

"I told you this guy was kooky," Timmy said to Dirty Dick Daryl while pointing at me with his thumb.

"Yeah, he is. You know, you're alright," Dirty Dick Daryl said to me.

They were silly putty in my hand. I needed patience before I pounded the fuck out of them.

On the way to the theater, these losers hammed it up as if they actually had words of substance.

"Did you get the tickets for *A Rainbow For Harriet* like you were supposed to, Dirty Dick?" Davy asked.

"Dude, I Fandangoed the shit out of the fucking movie. We're in, dudes. Which reminds me, I'm going to need to get the money from you guys."

"I don't have any money on me right now, but I think I'll have it for you tomorrow," Davy said.

"Don't even look at me, Daryl, I've paid you back through weed so many times that this one's on you," Timmy said. Dirty Dick Daryl looked at me.

"Um, I'm broke. I will, uh, holler at you tomorrow, dawg," I said.

"You cheap ass motherfuckers better pay me back tomorrow or else I'm cock-slapping you across each of your faces. I don't even know what kind of diseases I got on my dick, but I know it ain't good, and I think I'm dyin' as a result. I can't be droppin' Franklins like this and not be paid back! Movies aren't cheap, you know! How much of an allowance do you think I get?"

When we got to the movie theater, Dirty Dick Daryl picked up the tickets for *A Rainbow for Harriet* while the rest of us stood by the concession stand.

"Look, the movie starts at four-fifteen, but *Taco Bell: THE MOVIE* starts at four twenty-five. We'll walk past the ticket dude and then walk right into *Taco Bell: THE MOVIE* as if we own the fucking place," Timmy said.

"I would love to own a movie theater someday," Davy said.

"Shut the fuck up, Davy," Timmy said. "By the way, I have a surprise for you guys. When we get inside, I say we smoke this fat fuck." He pulled out a Ziploc bag full of those marijuanas I told you about earlier in the story. My eyes beamed at the bag.

"Where'd you get that? I thought you wouldn't have any until tomorrow…" I said to him.

"I always have a stash, Coop. I'm a drug dealer, duh," he said, and laughed with his goons.

I wanted to shove my whole forearm up his scrawny ass and pull out his intestines. He had some nerve to make me look like a fool and deny me my pot originally. I had just about enough of it and punched the motherfucker in the face. You should have seen his puny ass fall to the ground. He started crying immediately. He shut the fuck up when I gave him a roundhouse kick to the head, knocking him unconscious.

I then looked at Davy and said, "Woof," as I kicked him in the testicles, followed by the throat with the heel of my right foot. Dante and Dale came at me. I poked Dale in the eye, and almost removed it from its disgusting socket. I hit him directly on his stomach's pressure point. He swarmed around on the floor screaming in pain. I then dislocated Dante's arm, put him in a headlock, and ran his head straight into a wall as hard as I could. I then snapped Dwayne's right arm in half and karate-chopped his neck as hard as I could. He fell to the floor like forty-five pounds of wet shit in a sack. I stepped on his head as he was lying and screaming in pain and lunged at Derek. The foolish fuck pulled a knife out. I grabbed coins from my pocket and threw them at his face. That caught him off-guard. I punched him square in the forehead, and then shoved the bone of his nose straight up through his brain. I killed him. That showed that motherfucker for pulling a knife out on me. Dustin's jaw dropped to the ground. He couldn't believe what was going on. I walked up to him, spit in his face, picked him up with both my arms, and gave him a backbreaker. Dirty Dick Daryl appeared out of nowhere with a gun and badge drawn.

"Put your fucking arms in the air! You're under arrest! I'm an undercover cop!" He yelled.

I should have put two and two together. I should have known that 'Dirty Dick' Daryl meant that he was a detective. I should have remembered him as being Earl Hutchins, in the undercover unit at Middleton for twenty years. I even met him at the holiday party. I should have also remembered that I'm an ex-Navy Seal, so I shouldn't have been so excessive with these kids. I should have also realized that I was in my mid-forties, and that these kids were on average sixteen years old. I should have then realized that I should have ended my rampage after Dirty Dick Daryl revealed himself to be an undercover officer. Instead, I kicked his gun out of his hand and tackled him to the ground. I began to pound my bloody right fist against his cranium and crushed his testicles with my left hand. The screams of agonizing pain, paired with the blood on my face, kind of deafened and blinded me from what was really going on around me. Parents, children, teenagers, and pregnant concession stand cashiers were surrounding the gruesome scene.

I began to scream at the top of my lungs, "You motherfuckers have got nothing on me! I'm going to see you assholes rot in prison! You're getting fucked in the ass by me before you even get there! Your lives are fucked from now on, all eight of you! Good, law-abiding, reasonable gentlemen like me always win! You eight scumbags will rot for the rest of your pathetic lives in jail cells! I'll make a personal visit to each of your jail cells and fuck each of you physically and metaphorically! One of my fingers up each one of your eight asses! One in the pink, eight in the stink! One in the pink, eight in the stink!"

I don't really recall what happened immediately afterwards, but the next thing I remember after screaming at the top of my lungs at the theater was waking up in a hospital room. I was told that I was in a coma for two months. I was also told that while I was beating the fuck out of Dirty Dick Daryl, some rookie shot me in the back of the head with his gun. It did some damage to my brain, naturally. Anyway, police officers surrounded my hospital bed and revealed to me that I had killed Dale, Dante, and Derek. I was also notified that Dustin would be paralyzed for life after the backbreaker I had given him. Dwayne had nerve damage on his neck, causing him to be unable to fully bend his arms for the rest of his life. Good luck to him in writing those letters to Cat Fancy. Earl Hutchins, a.k.a. Dirty Dick Daryl, was in a coma for two weeks after I was through with him – or rather before a bullet was lodged in the back of my head. I was told that Timmy and Davy walked away with bruises. The sons of bitches eluded me! Both of their families sued me after the encounter. I was told I was being charged with manslaughter, so what the fuck did I care that I was being sued?

I was given life imprisonment, and have been in this jail cell for six years. I occasionally get letters from Davy that just read, 'Fuck you,' accompanied with pictures of himself masturbating on the letter he had written (and that I held to read) before he stuffed it in the envelope. I realize now that I shouldn't have gone too far with the police brutality. But, I do have a bad temper that I still need to learn to suppress.

While in my jail cell, I keep to myself and think about what an asset I was out on the streets, and about what the matter is with kids today. No one took the effort to stop drug trafficking in Monroe as seriously as I did. Everyone else was — and still is — asleep at the wheel.

Timmy was exonerated from the drug counts on the basis that there wasn't enough evidence against him. I was also told that I foiled Earl Hutchins' investigation thanks to my little outbreak. Middleton Police Department's undercover unit was developing a huge case against Timmy, but the investigation was thwarted after my attack. People actually started to pity these fucking teenagers. I was like, 'For real and shit?'.

I hear that there's now a major drug epidemic on the streets of Monroe as I sit in a jail cell, hum Howlin' Howard & the Mamma's Boys songs to myself, and read letters from punks I've crossed paths with in my previous life. Society is deteriorating outside these walls. One thing's always certain, though. I ain't never touching a fucking marijuana. That shit ruins lives.

TOM CRUISE ATE HERE ONCE

**Table 1 – David & Moira**

The restaurant was inhabited with its weekend crowd. David was convinced the floor was rumbling due to the tremors caused by his right leg quickly shaking up and down uncontrollably at the table. He felt like his dinner from two days ago would come out through his mouth. He hadn't been able to eat a full meal in days. This was the most nervous he could recall ever being.

"Rafael, you still have it, right?" David asked.

"Relax, Mister David. You're going crazy and starting to scare poor Rafael. Everything is under control. You do your part and Rafael will do his. You and Rafael have gone over this six times," Rafael responded.

"I over-prepare; it's what I do. I can't help it. Could you please go over it once more so I know we're on the same page?"

"You and Rafael have been on the same page for six pages now. The book you're reading is bigger than the Koran. So many pages."

"Now's not the day to fuck with me, Rafael. Yesterday was a day you could have done it. I'm wide open to be fucked with tomorrow. Why don't I come by around noon so you could have me the whole afternoon? Today, though, is terrible timing. I'm sorry for cursing. It's an incredibly nerve-racking day for me. Now you think I'm a dick because I just snapped at you, and that gives me something else to worry about because I try so hard for people to like me."

"Relax, Mister David. Drink more water. Breathe. Calm down. Your leg is going to cause our patrons' food to fall off their plates. The elderly lady at table eleven is already talking about shakes at her table, but Rafael told her it might very well be her dementia. It's ok for Rafael to joke about that with her. Anyway, Rafael will walk you through it again to ensure everything is perfectly under control. When Miss Moira comes, you two will order the Barbaresco, since it was what you drank on your first date two years ago. It also reminds her of her father on Thanksgiving nights when she was little because he would drink it at the dinner table, get drunk, and dance with her, her sister, and mother to Beatles songs in the living room. They particularly danced to the love songs. Her favorite to dance with her father to was *I Will*, sung by Paul McCartney, off the White Album."

"I told you all that stuff? I don't remember telling you that."

"Oh, but you did, the fourth time you and Rafael went through it to make sure you were *on the same page*. Rafael does not make up stories, or else his name would be Estephen King. Don't interrupt, please. You make yourself look stupid when you do."

"Alright, go on. Sorry."

"So, Rafael will bring you the wine and pour it, cuing you to bring up her father and the dancing in the living room when she was younger. You will order the dessert first because that was what you did on your first date as well."

"I was such a clown back then. I mean, ordering dessert first? Who does that?" David interrupted.

"Interrupting again, Mister David? Didn't Rafael already tell you how stupid it makes you look? Why do you always want to look stupid? A man who's about to propose to a woman wants to look like a wise man. Not an idiot who always interrupts," Rafael said.

David mimed zipping his lips together and throwing away the key.

"Thank you for throwing that key away, Mister David. Now, where was Rafael? Oh, yes, when Rafael comes out with the dessert, he will have the engagement ring on the middle of the tray. Rafael will say, 'We only have one cannoli for the gentleman, but we have this ring on-hand for the lovely lady.' Then Rafael will say that there was no pun intended when he brought this out and said 'on-hand,' cuing you to sarcastically say, 'Yeah, right.' Rafael will then place the box with the ring by you, where you will then take a big gulp of the wine, get down on one knee, and ask for her hand in marriage. When she accepts, Rafael and company will be there to applaud, and so will the whole restaurant. Rafael will also get you a round of Diet Cokes, on the house, as a form of congratulations."

"Yes, please make sure to really be loud about the free Diet Cokes. That's pretty cool. It sounds like you took good mental notes. Thank you so much."

"What time should Rafael be expecting her, Mister David?"

"I think within the next ten to fifteen minutes. She texted me saying she was getting into her car. She only works about ten minutes from here with good traffic."

"Ok, so you and Rafael are in order. Do you want Rafael to go through it again for an eighth time?"

"No, I think that's fine. You've got it down. Sorry I was so annoying. This is a big day for me."

"Of course, Mister David, of course! Good luck. If you need anything, Rafael will only be a few feet away."

David had been planning for this day for three months. He worked overtime at the customer service center to make enough money to pay for it. It wasn't cheap. That evening was his two-year anniversary with Moira. He was at first unsure of whether his engagement should be made a into spectacle in front of so many people, but he thought it would add to the memorable experience.

He threw up a little in his mouth when Moira walked through the entrance. It was a pastrami sandwich he ate two days prior. He was so nervous that it seemed like the food he ate days ago never digested because his stomach and intestines were tied in knots.

"Hi, here, let me help you with your seat," he said as he got up and pulled the chair out for her.

"Thanks. Today was so crazy. So many people needed emergency root canals. I must have booked six appointments for today alone, and one woman called me a camel's cunt for not penciling her in. I've never been called a cunt before, let alone a camel's cunt. Today was unreal."

"That's not nice. Well, happy anniversary."

"Wait, is today our? Wait, oh, my goodness, it is! I totally forgot! I've been so wrapped up in what's been going on at work, that thing my parents are going through, and the cooking class. I lost track of days. It actually made me want to talk to you about things as well," she said as tears started building in her eye sockets. David didn't notice.

"Hold that thought. I see the waiter," David said, ignoring the latter part of what Moira said. "Sir, please bring us the Barbaresco."

"As you wish," Rafael said.

"Please, my girlfriend and I don't like to wait, so chop-chop."

Rafael gave David a stern look. He had gone off the script.

"Ese pendejo. Hijo de puta," Rafael whispered to himself.

"That sucks about being called a camel cunt. How rude. That is so…so rude," David said.

"I'm afraid that's not the worst of it, though," Moira said as she started wiping her tears. David didn't realize she was gently sobbing.

"Oh, no? What happened that was worse?"

"I think we should talk about it after we eat."

"Oh, it's that bad, huh? I *really* want to hear all about this."

"Yeah, so, uh, how was your day?"

"Oh, I did a little running around."

"What does that mean?"

"I had a lot of errands to run."

"Yeah, but what did you have to do? You know, you never tell me anything anymore. We hardly ever speak. I tell you about my day, and you pretty much just skirt over telling me about yours."

"There's not much to say about my day."

"I know, I've noticed because you don't ever talk to me anymore."

"What do you want me to say?"

"Well, anything would be a start."

"Alright, alright, let's cool our jets here. You've had a long day, and you'll feel better after a nice meal. It's our anniversary."

"Stop patronizing me. I'm sick of it. And don't use our anniversary as a tool for your advantage."

"What are you talking about?"

Rafael walked over to them with a bottle of Barbaresco.

"Who's thirsty?" Rafael said with a grin stretching from ear to ear, exposing the slight gap between his two front teeth. "Rafael had this brought over from the motherland just for you!" He saw the look on both their faces. He decided to loosen the mood. "Who wants to see Rafael perform some magic tricks, eh?"

"Not right now, Rafael, please," David said, with a look that screamed of urgency. Rafael poured wine into their glasses and walked back to the kitchen. He didn't know what was happening, but decided to bring out the cannoli and the ring in order to sooth the mood.

"Tito, one cannoli, ASAP!" He yelled to the pastry chef. "Make this one extra-sweet. Rafael's got a couple getting married!"

"Aye, that's all you had to say! I'll make this one extra especial," Tito responded.

"On Rafael's watch, this is going to be a truly memorable engagement," Rafael said to himself. "Mister David will remember the name Rafael for the rest of his life."

Back at the table, David was trying to calm Moira.

"Please, let's just enjoy this meal. Remember two years ago at this time? I knew back then you were special. You were – and still are – the most beautiful woman these sorry eyes have ever looked at. While I know I haven't been open or available, as you've clearly stated, I know it's something that's easily rectifiable. You are the light that gives me the energy to go throughout my life. You are my beacon of hope in my own humanity. Honey, I love you."

Moira began to cry. She grabbed a napkin and covered her face as she sobbed into it. David, assuring himself that she was crying because of the poignant words he said to her, felt good about himself and thought that he still had *it*. He got up to give her a hug.

"There, there," he said as he embraced her. She didn't respond. The gesture made her sob more. He became embarrassed as they started receiving attention from the other patrons. He looked towards Rafael and nodded his head while mouthing the phrase, 'the ring.' Rafael gave a confident nod and quickly walked into the kitchen.

"Tito, the cannoli, we need the cannoli now. It is time. The time has come. Now is the zero hour. There is no time like the present,"

Rafael said as he was thinking of other 'present time' clichés.

"Aye, déjame a respirar por un segundo! Here, here is the cannoli. No more rushing for tonight, ok?" Tito responded.

"A masterpiece, as always," Rafael said as he grabbed Tito by the back of the head and brought it forward to plant a kiss on his cheek.

"Oye, maricón, I told you to not do that anymore!" Tito said.

"Oh, behave, it's just an act of appreciation."

"You know, there are other ways to show this appreciation."

"No time to discuss now, Rafael has an engagement to celebrate."

As he walked towards to kitchen door, Rafael placed the tray with the cannoli on a small table, reached into the inside pocket of his blazer, and pulled out the ring. He placed it on the tray.

"David, I think I need to go," Moira said.

"Nonsense, let's stay here and enjoy our meal. Look, here comes the waiter!"

"Rafael saw you were in a sad mood, so he brought this cannoli out. Unfortunately, this one is for the gentleman, but Rafael does have this ring on-hand. There is no pun intended by Rafael saying 'on-hand' with the ring," Rafael said.

"Yeah, right!" David said as he winked.

"What?" Moira said as she saw David grab the ring from the tray and get down on one knee.

"Moira, honey, darling, sweetheart. You mean the world to me. I never want to leave that world. I want to live in it forever, which is why I want to ask – will you marry me?"

A sudden hush fell upon the restaurant. Everyone stopped what they were doing, and all eyes were on the two of them. Moira was visibly shaking. She looked at the ring, at Rafael, and at David in succession three times. She noticed how large the restaurant was, and how many people were staring at her. She looked at David and whispered, "I can't…"

"What, dear?" David said, not believing her response.

"I don't think I love you. I've been trying to tell you that, and that's what I wanted to talk to you about. You've made this whole situation into a spectacle, and I apologize that it's not the reaction you wanted. I'm so, so sorry for that. I have too much going on in my life right now – with work, my parents, and stuff that I want to do for myself. I'm twenty-six years old. I'm not ready for marriage, and I don't think I want to be with anyone right now. The thought of a lifelong commitment is something I don't think I need or am ready for at this stage in my life. I'm so sorry, David. You're a wonderful person, I truly mean that, but I don't want to marry you. I'm so sorry to you, your family, and your friends. I haven't been happy in some time, and I'm sorry I put on this charade for the past few months. I have to go. I'm so sorry, everyone. I'm so sorry to you, David. You have every right to hate me, and I hate myself for not being able to make this evening the magical one you had hoped for. I'm not that person for you. I'm not even sure I know who or what I am for myself. I feel so stupid. Here I go fucking something else up. I forgot our anniversary, I feel like a failure to my parents, have a dead-end job where I was cursed out in the most awful way today, and now I can't give you what you want. I have to go," she said as she got up. David grabbed her by the arm.

"No, wait, please, don't – " David said.

"Let me go, David." He didn't let her go.

"Let me go, David," she repeated.

"But, I love you…"

"David, let me go! Let me go now! Let go of my fucking arm!" She screamed. "I want to get out of this fucking place! David, let me go!"

He let her go. She ran out of the restaurant. David sat in the chair she had sat in. His eyes gazed at the front entrance while twirling the engagement ring between his right index and middle fingers. The restaurant was still silent until one person chuckled faintly towards the back and tried to cover it up with a cough.

"Mister David, the bottle and cannoli are on us. Don't you worry about it, ok?" Rafael said.

David didn't answer.

"Everyone, please continue to enjoy your meals. No more show here. Please, let Rafael and his friend here have a moment. Thank you," Rafael said to the patrons. Things slowly returned back to normal.

"What the fuck happened?" David asked. Rafael wasn't sure if that was a rhetorical question.

"Give her some time to be by herself. You never know. She may need some time on her own before she gets back to you," Rafael said as he put his hand on David's shoulder. David started to cry. He put his hand on top of Rafael's hand.

"I have to go. I've made myself look like enough of a dick in front of everyone. I'm going to hold on to this for a few days," he said, looking at the engagement ring. "If she doesn't come back to me, I could always return it and get my money back. Shit, this is a day I'll remember until the day I die. Thanks for your help, Rafael. I know I was annoying, but thank you. Thank you so much."

He got up and hugged Rafael. He was crying harder than Moira had.

"It's ok, Mister David. Everything will be ok. You will be stronger after this. She is stressed. Let her rest, and you will see what happens. If she comes back, then you come back here, and Rafael will take care of everything. Does that sound good to you?"

"You're right. She needs some time to cool down. I'll reach out to her in a few days and see what's going on. I think there's been enough time since she left. Think I'll run into her in the parking lot?"

"Doubtful. Go home and rent that Matt Damon movie where he's a poker player. It's on Netflix."

"*Rounders.*"

"*Rounders?*"

"That's the Matt Damon movie you're talking about. The poker movie with Matt Damon and Edward Norton. It's called *Rounders*," David said.

"No, Rafael believes it's called *Good Will Hunting*. He's good at poker and his name is Will Hunting, so he's *Good Will Hunting*. You need to see it. Rafael saw it the other night, and it made him feel better."

David wasn't sure which Matt Damon movie to watch now. He hadn't seen either of them. He decided he'd watch both, hoping they'd make him feel better.

"Thank you, Rafael."

"Go home, Mister David. Sleep it off. Tomorrow is a new day."

David hugged Rafael once more and slowly walked towards the front exit. He looked at the people in the restaurant as he was making his way towards the door. Each person looked much happier than him. He was convinced every single person there had someone thinking about each of them and were genuinely happy with their lives. He was jealous of all of them. He saw a couple with their children who looked like they were out of a Norman Rockwell painting, two beautiful girls who were most likely in love with the men they were with, a young man and woman engaged in deep, loving-like conversation with each other. That used to be, and could have still been, him and Moira. He wanted that. When he walked to the door, he took one last look at everyone living their blissful lives in the establishment, knowing his was far from it. He felt a depression that surged throughout his body. He sighed and walked out.

### Table 2 – Michael & Travis

"Whoa, tough break for that guy, right?" Michael said.

"What a way to rip a guy's heart out of his chest. You think he's gonna kill himself?" Travis asked.

"I hope not. I know I'd have been depressed if Christina denied me when I proposed to her."

"Oh, yeah? I remember when you were feeling that depression the time Danielle Palmer gave Arnold Bernard a handjob."

Michael almost spit out the wine he was drinking.

"That's a name I haven't thought about in years. I remember that," Michael said. "She gave him a handjob over the chip bowl at Derek Weisman's house party. What was the nickname she got after that?"

"Dani Arnold-Palmer," Travis responded. "And I still ate those fucking chips after she – or shall I say he – was finished. Didn't even need dip for them either."

"That's so gross!" Michael said and laughed. "Wow, Danielle Palmer. I wonder what she's doing now."

"Who cares? Girls come and girls go. We were used to that."

"Yeah, girls weren't into us, but I was lucky to eventually find someone. I couldn't be happier with her and my two girls."

"Yeah, you're living it up as father and husband. How old are your kids again?"

"Audrey is three and Angie is six."

"I can't believe it. Mikey Donner married with kids. I'm surprised you're a family man. I remember the two of us swore to hate women and their idiot boyfriends and husbands forever."

"Yeah, well, we were young and naïve. We thought we had the world figured out then. We were kids."

"We were kids who were exposed to the real world earlier than normal people. We experienced the bullshit."

"I don't agree with that."

"Eh, whatever. I've had too many sips of this wine. I gotta eat more casserole to slow it down. What are you doing for your birthday tomorrow?"

"I'm thinking of taking Christina and the kids to the beach. It's supposed to be a nice one tomorrow. Last year, Christina planned a surprise party for me. I'm hoping this year will be a quiet one. Your birthday is tomorrow, too. What are you going to be doing?"

"I'm surprised you remembered we shared the same birthday."

"Of course! How could I forget?"

"Never forget we share the same birthday and age. Remember that. Same birthday and age. We turn forty tomorrow. Fucking forty!"

"As if I don't feel old already. Why don't you stay the night, and we'll celebrate both our birthdays tomorrow? I doubt Christina will mind. It's not like I see you every day. It's been how long again? You told me before, but I still can't believe it!"

"Nineteen years."

"You tell me that, and it seems like that long, but I still find it incredibly hard to believe."

"You've been living a pretty successful life. Wife, kids, partner at the firm, so I'd imagine time flew by for you."

"Yeah, man. I busted my ass for years, but anyone else could have done it, too."

"I wish I had that determination, Mikey. Do people call you Mikey at work?"

"No, they call me Michael."

"Well, to me, you'll always be Mikey."

"Well, we do go back a long time."

"No shit! We'd get drunk, smoke some dope, and listen to The Fucking Smiths, The Fucking Cure, and when Cobain committed suicide, we listened to fucking Nirvana."

"What kid didn't go through a Nirvana phase back then?"

"Anyway, we'd bitch about girls, think our lives were cursed, hated our parents, hated school, hated our town, trapped in a fucking cell of a life."

Michael was becoming uncomfortable.

"What about you, Travis? We haven't really been talking about you. What have you been up to? I was shocked to get a message from you last week. I'm really glad you reached out. I've missed you."

"Missed me? I think you're the first person to say that to me. I've been living my life as usual. I'm fixing bikes."

"Oh, cool. I think motorcycles are great. I've been thinking about getting one if Christina allows me to. They're dangerous, so I don't want her to worry about me whenever I'd go out on one."

"Not a fucking motorcycle. I mean a fucking bike. Like a bicycle."

"Oh, sorry. I'm planning on getting Angie her first bike for her birthday in a few months."

"Well, ain't that the fucking life for her," Travis said as he took another gulp of his wine.

Rafael stopped at the table.

"How are the gentlemen doing?" Rafael asked as he picked up their plates.

"We're running low on the wine. Get us another of this, what's it called? Sacco?" Travis said.

"Saracco Moscato d'Asti," Rafael answered.

"Yes, could we please have another bottle of that?" Michael asked.

"Could Rafael interest you in the dessert menu?" Rafael asked.

"Definitely," Michael said.

"Before you bring out the dessert, the booze needs to be doing more of its job, so, chop-chop," Travis said.

"As you wish, sir," Rafael said. "Ese pendejo. Hijo de puta," he whispered to himself as he walked away.

"So, where were we?" Michael asked.

"My pathetic life fixing bicycles," Travis answered.

"No, it's not pathetic in the least bit. You're a great guy, Travis."

"Spare me. You don't need to try to make me feel better. It's all a waste of breath anyway. There's a reason why I reached out to you after all these years."

Rafael interrupted with another bottle of wine and the dessert menu.

"That was fuckin' fast," Travis said.

"Rafael takes pride in his service," Rafael said.

"Yeah, I could see you have a lot of pride. Where's your rainbow pin?" Travis said.

"Rafael does not understand."

Michael felt the urge to intervene.

"Please excuse my friend. He's had too much wine. Please give us a minute to decide on the dessert. Thanks so much," Michael said.

"As you wish," Rafael said and walked to another table.

"Listen, man, you need to cool it with that talk. We're not teenagers anymore testing people's reactions. We're grown men," Michael said to Travis.

"Fuck off, man. Listen, we don't have to spend our limited time here arguing."

"Alright. Then, please compose yourself. I come in here sometimes with my family. The last thing I need is someone manipulating my food."

"You mean jerk off in it? That what you mean by *manipulating*?"

"Yes, that is exactly what I mean. The last thing I need is my wife eating another guy's, you know, stuff."

"Or your kids…"

"Stop right there, Travis. I will not – "

"Relax, relax, I was kidding. People don't really jerk off in people's food anyway, unless you're at Denny's or something. This place doesn't look like the type to do that. You got Yelp, Twitter, and all that internet shit these days, anyway. They don't wanna risk the bad press."

"Just calm down and watch what you say. I'm coming real close to decking you in the mouth. I won't like it, and you'll likely kick my ass after I do it, but I just want to drive the point by decking you in the mouth that I don't like it."

"This is the old Mikey I've been missing. This is the guy I've been waiting for the past nineteen years! I knew he was still alive."

"I don't do like ninety-nine percent of the things I used to do when we used to hang out."

"Like what, smoke weed?"

"No, I don't do that, and I don't sniff glue anymore either."

"Now, that's surprising."

"I think I killed like a thousand brain cells by doing that sort of shit."

"You're living the good life. Not sniffing glue and paying for stuff to jerk off to with your own money, I bet, too. I wish I had that. I still do it to the image of Victoria Sanchez. Remember her?"

"Why are you constantly reliving the old days? You still

masturbate to Victoria Sanchez? That was when we were like thirteen. Remember the time we saw her showering from Lucas' bedroom window?"

"She didn't give a fuck that window was wide open and we were watching from her neighbor's room. She didn't even have the fucking shower curtain closed."

"I think it was more memorable watching her slip all around that wet floor because she showered with the curtain open."

"It's because she knew we were looking. I shoulda run out to that bathroom and fucked her in that shower. I'm so stupid! I shoulda done that!" Travis said, and then punched himself once in the head. Michael became even more uncomfortable and concerned.

"Yeah, well, that's all behind us now – decades behind us. Maybe you should look her up."

"Nah, she's dead."

"Really? She died? How?"

"Complications from birth. The baby died, too."

"That's awful."

"Yeah, I'm jealous of the baby."

"What? That's a terrible thing to say!"

"How? That baby didn't waste its time. Too much bullshit going on, and people are just scumbags. Victoria also didn't waste any time dying young."

"You have a weird, warped view of the world, Travis."

"It's the same one it's always been, and you used to share it with me."

"*Used to.* I grew up, and it sounds like you need to as well. I don't think that way anymore. That doesn't go to say that I regret how I thought in the past. Being young is all about liking what you like at the time, and not at all thinking about whether you'll feel the same way when you get older."

"Funny you mention that part about having no regrets about stuff that happened in the past."

"No, why would I have regrets? We had fun times back then."

"Back to why I reached out to you before the waiter interrupted us. Do you remember the freshman spring dance, back in high school?"

"No, not really."

"We got there, but no one wanted us there, so we got fucked up under Heller's Bridge. That's when you told me about when your old man died when you were little."

"I don't remember that at all, but I must have told you."

"Yeah, anyway, you got all sad and shit, and you hated the way your life was going. I hated the way mine was, too. We knew we had a connection because we shared the same birthday. We had enough of this shitty place. We had nowhere to go but six feet under. And we realized that was where we should ultimately be – as with every other fucking scumbag in that shithole town we grew up in."

"What's your point, Travis? I'm getting tired of this."

"That's right, you're a lawyer now. Cut to the point, right? Anyway, we talked about committing suicide that night. I'm the one who had to stop it. I remember that. You wanted to climb the bridge and jump off. You actually started to climb it, and I had to pull you down. You don't remember this?"

The night had been so deeply buried inside Michael that he had forgotten about it, but the description sounded vaguely familiar.

"I think I'm starting to," Michael said.

"I said that this life, despite it being shitty, must have something in store for us. I said that since we were only in our teens, we had the bullshit handed to us early, and then the rest of our lives would be smooth sailing. I refused to believe that was all that life had to offer. Fast-forward to today, and it turns out I was wrong. You were so into doing it, though. You even tried to climb the bridge a second time! I thought I'd have to tackle you to the ground and beat you down. That's how determined you were to ending it that night. I thought of a compromise, though. I told you that we should continue to move on, and that if this rotten world was still rotten after some time, then we'd do it together – and that I wouldn't be stopping you that time. We made a pact, and even went as far as to signing this," Travis said.

He pulled out a piece of paper from his pocket. It was folded neatly, yet it was wrinkled and had what appeared to be dried blood all over it.

"That night, we went to my house and wrote this note, this promise to ourselves. This paper, which I've held on to for over two decades, states that we would commit a joint suicide on our fortieth birthday. You and I share a birthday, Mikey, and it's stated here – which we both signed with our fucking blood, literally – that if one of us still wants to go on with it, then we would *both* do it. Look at the date. It's tomorrow. So, Mikey, I reached out to you after nineteen years of not speaking to you, to come collect. I came here to end it all with you as we promised. We have a pact we need to honor."

It all came back to Michael as he saw the note. His mouth dropped wide open and his eyes were fixed on the note as Travis placed it on the table. Rafael returned to take their dessert order.

"Anything Rafael could get you for dessert?"

"The tiramisu…" Michael said in a low voice, eyes still fixed on the note.

"As you wish, sir. And for you?" Rafael asked Travis.

"Nothing. I'm good. Thanks, chief," he said as he poured himself another glass of wine.

"One tiramisu coming up," Rafael said.

"So, whatcha thinking about? You know a vow is a vow. You're a lawyer. I have it here in writing," Travis said

"A vow is a vow, you're right, but that particular note is not a binding contract. We wrote that as teenagers, under the influence of drugs and alcohol. And besides, it's a fucking *suicide* contract."

"Yeah, I know, but you said it. A vow is a vow. You made a promise, Mikey. And, if it weren't for me, you'd be dead by now anyway."

"Yeah, well, I'm not. I have a different life now. That's been established, what, like at least a dozen times now?"

"It doesn't fucking matter. You made a promise, written in your own blood. You owe me your life."

"I have to use the restroom," Michael said, and got up from the table. "Don't eat my tiramisu while I'm gone."

Michael noticed his hands were shaking and clammy when he opened the restroom door.

"Good evening, sir," the restroom attendant said.

"Hey…" Michael replied. "Um, I'm going to wash my face. Is that ok?"

"Why, of course, sir," the attendant replied.

"Thanks."

Michael walked to the sink and began to wet his face. He didn't want to look at his reflection in the mirror. He wanted to sneak out through the window, but knew that would add to the weirdness of the evening.

"How strong is a bond?" He asked the attendant.

"Come again?"

"How strong is a bond – your word? A promise?"

"A bond is the strongest thing a man could ever have. Without a man's word, what is he? What does he have to account for himself?"

"Even if he made a bond as a teenager?"

"A teenager?"

"I made a suicide pact with a friend of mine when I was like fourteen or something. He's come to collect my life."

"Suicide pact? Suicide is just as cowardly as hitting a woman. A suicide pact made at fourteen is something that makes me believe you were a coward back then. And being uncertain whether that bond you made at fourteen still holds today as a man in your, I would guess forties, makes you stupid – probably just as much as you were when you were fourteen making suicide pacts."

"You are the wisest restroom attendant I have ever met. Do you know that?"

"I got my Ph.D. from Yale, sir."

"What's your name?"

"Raul, sir."

"Thank you, Raul. Thank you very much," Michael said as he handed Raul a twenty-dollar bill.

Michael walked back to the table. His tiramisu was waiting for him.

"Everything come out ok? Still got some poop in your chute?" Travis asked.

"The bathroom attendant said I shouldn't kill myself with you."

"I *knew* you'd pussy out! This is such bullshit! You're gonna make me do it on my own, aren't you? I thought we were fucking friends."

"Look, we made that pact when we were teenagers. We were fucking teenagers! *Listen* to what I'm telling you."

"Look at what I'm *showing* you," Travis said and pulled out the paper again. "Look at your signature. I didn't forge that shit. It's legit!"

"Everything is different now. And if things changed for me, they will change for you."

"Alright, there, Mister Dali Lama. I thought I came here for a reason, but it looks like I wasted my last full fucking day."

"It doesn't have to be this way. Look, how about you stay with me for a bit? Where are you staying while you're in town?"

"I'm staying someplace, don't you worry about where I'm staying. I won't accept your charity. I'm gonna go through with what I said I'd do years ago because I'm no fucking pussy or liar. My word is all I've got, and it's the most solid shit anyone's ever got. You were a genuine dude who spoke his mind and did his shit. Now you just are shit. I'm glad I got to realize this now."

"You're not going to die, Travis. Stop talking like an idiot."

"Look at yourself, you buttoned-up sucker. Are you really happy with your life? Your wife telling you whether you can get a motorcycle? Not sure if you could go to the beach on your own fucking birthday? What kind of shit is that?"

"I'm content with my life. I have people who love me. And so do you," Michael said as he reached out to touch Travis' arm.

"Get your fucking hand off me!" Travis yelled and got up from his chair. The patrons in the restaurant grew silent for a second time that evening.

"Oh, no. Not more drama," Rafael said as he heard Travis yell from the kitchen.

"What's going on out there?" Tito asked.

"The two gay gentlemen who had the casserole are arguing."

Michael continued to try calming Travis.

"Please sit down. Let's talk this through," Michael said.

"Fuck you and fuck everyone here. I'm outta this shithole," Travis said as he walked away.

"Travis, stop," Michael said and grabbed him by the arm again. Travis turned and punched Michael square in the face, causing him to fall on the floor and bleed from his nose.

"Let this scene be etched in your head for the rest of your life, asshole. Hopefully you won't forget it, like you did our pact. You'll be reading about me real soon," Travis said as he walked out of the restaurant. He looked at Alejandra, the hostess. "You wanna get one next, motherfucker?"

Alejandra moved out of the way to let him pass.

Rafael helped Michael up.

"He was the second person to storm out of here tonight. What's wrong with Rafael's food?"

"Could you shut the fuck up, get me some napkins, and call me an ambulance?" Michael said.

Rafael handed him napkins to wipe the blood from his face. Michael walked out of the restaurant and waited for the ambulance on the curb. Rafael followed him outside.

"You don't have to worry about the bill. Rafael saw the lovers' quarrel. Rafael is very sorry. It is the second time tonight a relationship has ended here. Is there a full moon out?" Rafael asked.

"The fuck are you talking about, lovers' quarrel? He was my friend from childhood."

"Then what was he so angry about?"

"Just fuck off and go back inside."

"Rafael gives you two a free meal and this is what Rafael gets?"

"Fuck off before I do to you what he did to me."

Rafael walked back inside. Michael looked at his hands. He noticed blood between his fingers, and stretched it out as he separated his index and middle ones. He started writing on the pavement with the blood on his fingertips. He had finished writing 'Nirvana' when the ambulance arrived at the parking lot.

### Table 3 – Anthony & Michelle

Michelle was sickened by the amount of blood she saw coming out of the man's nose, who was getting into the back of the ambulance. She wanted to look away, but couldn't. Even if she tried, the siren lights dancing in the shadows would remind her that a scene was taking place just feet away from her. She made glances at what was going on, and at her watch. He was late. She thought that she should have been late, but there was no turning back. She couldn't leave and come back again. That would have seemed desperate, even to herself. The ambulance began to drive away. She realized that it was odd that no one escorted the man into it. She was beginning to lose her appetite when she saw 'Nirvana' written on the pavement in blood. She was thinking it could be a bad sign, and that she should get into her car and drive away. However, she was interested in meeting him. Even though she was telling herself one thing, her head was saying something else. He was officially seventeen minutes late. She told herself she'd give him another thirteen minutes. Soon after, she heard and saw a car peel into the parking lot. It was a BMW. The car parked a few feet away from where the ambulance had been stationed. She couldn't make out if the man getting out of the car was him. He approached her and looked at his cell phone.

"Hey, you Michelle?" He asked.

"Yes. Are you Anthony?" She asked.

"The one and only. Like what you see?"

"I guess…" She said, not knowing how else to respond.

"You don't look so different from your profile. Check it out," he said as he showed Michelle her dating profile on his phone.

"Yeah, you're right, that's certainly me."

"And I approve. Me-wow!"

"So, um, should we go inside?"

"Yeah, of course. Lemme lock up my kitten first," he said as he pressed the lock on his keychain. The car played the lyric, *'Obey your master…'* from Metallica's *Master of Puppets*, from its speakers instead of beeping like a regular car typically does whenever the lock button is pressed on the keychain.

"Pretty sweet, right? I got my boy Richie to hook it up for me. I'm the only guy in the state – maybe even the country – who has that sort of setup. You into Metallica?" Anthony asked.

"No, can't say I am," Michelle said.

"Oh, no? What are you into? Linkin Park? Evanescence?"

"No, I don't know, Blondie, Talking Heads, David Bowie, that sort of stuff?"

"That's old man shit. I won't hold it against you, though, on account of you being so cute. Check it out," he said as he pointed to the word written in blood on the pavement. "Nirvana. What geezer wrote that? Go back to the nineties, gramps!"

"Wasn't Metallica popular in the nineties as well?"

"Metallica is timeless. They were popular in the eighties *and* nineties."

"Wouldn't that make them even older and more irrelevant compared to Nirvana by alluding to being outdated because they were popular in the nineties?"

"Huh?"

"Never mind. That's gross. It's written in blood. It's not even dry yet."

"Someone probably got beat up for liking shitty music," Anthony said as he scoffed.

Alejandra met them at the door as they stepped inside.

"How are you this evening?" Alejandra asked.

"Better than before," Anthony said with a grin.

Michelle was quickly reaching her limit. She was about to tell Anthony that she wasn't interested in continuing the date, but was startled by the sound of glass shattering on the floor. Someone at another table had dropped it in what she thought was a drunken stupor.

Alejandra walked the two of them to their table.

"Mind if I face the entrance? I like to scope out who's coming in and out," Anthony said.

"Sure..." Michelle responded.

"Yeah, I always check people out. It's a hobby of mine. Name me a guy who doesn't scope out chicks, right?"

"And you're planning on doing that tonight? Scope out *chicks* while you're on a date with me?"

"Nah, I'll be scoping you out throughout the night. I'll just be seeing your competition," he said as he looked up and down her chest.

"You just reminded me that I forgot my wallet in my car."

"Don't worry, hon, I've got you covered tonight. You don't need your wallet."

"I don't feel comfortable with it in my car. Someone could break into it just to get my wallet."

"Alright, if it's gonna make you crazy, I could let you do that."

"Thanks so much for allowing me to go to my own car to get my wallet," she said in a sarcastic tone.

"No worries."

If their water had been poured, she would have splashed it on his face. She then thought he wasn't worth the aggravation. She quickly looked through the menu.

"Do me a favor?" She asked.

"Anything, babe."

"Could you order me the lobster capellini with leek-tarragon cream sauce?" It was one of the more expensive items on the menu.

"Oh, sounds authentic. I'll get you that, sure, no problem."

"Great, thanks so much. I'll be right back," she said. She walked out of the restaurant, got into her car, and drove home.

Anthony ordered the steak carpaccio and San Pallegrino. It took him close to thirty minutes to realize she wasn't coming back.

## Table 4 – Betty, Chuck, Elizabeth, Scott

"I was literally hanging from the skin of my dick!" Chuck boasted. "I got the scars to prove it if you ever wanna 'em, Scotty!" He let out a bellicose laugh.

"Oh, ha-ha," Scott said nervously as he smiled.

"Oh, he's just teasing, honey. I told you Chuck was the crazy one at work," Betty said. "How do you put up with him, Elizabeth? I only have to deal with him for eight hours. You, on the other hand…"

"Oh, I'll show you how I've been putting up with him for twenty-seven years," Elizabeth said as she began to chug her wine. Some of it trickled down the side of her mouth. She wiped it and let out a mild burp.

"Damn straight that's how she puts up with me and Little Chuck. Oh, and our two-year-old-son, too! Ba-BAM!" Chuck said.

Seventy-five percent of the table erupted into laughter. Scott was uncomfortable.

"So, Scott, do you go out with your own coworkers at all, or do you usually tag along with Betty's?" Chuck asked while wiping tears from his eyes after laughing so hard at his own joke.

"Oh, well, I guess that'd be the case. I just go to work, do what I have to do, and then just – "

"I'm sorry, pal, snoozed in the middle of your sentence," Chuck said. The table erupted into laughter again. Scott became annoyed and felt embarrassed. "I'm just bustin' your balls, Scott. You got a pair, right? Lemme make sure," he said as he looked under the table at Scott's crotch. "Yup, they seem to be intact, but barely…"

"Yeah, well, allow me to duct tape them a little tighter in the restroom. If you'll excuse me," Scott said as he got up.

Scott walked to the men's room. He greeted the restroom attendant when he entered. As he stepped to the urinal, he heard a cell phone conversation a man was having in one of the stalls.

"Yeah, she totally dipped out. She was lame anyway. Her tits weren't as big as her frame could take. She coulda filled out her chest a little more. What? Yeah, bro! You're right. Yeah! Nah, man, it's pronounced *poon-na-nee*. What do you mean what am I gonna do next? Go home and jerk off to *Basic Instinct*. Yeah, I left it downloading before I left, so it should be ready by the time I get home. I hear it's awesome, and that the Sharon Stone scene where she crosses her legs – yeah, bro. Yeah, that's the scene I'm talking about! I'm squirtin' now just thinking about it! Alright, dude. Lemme wipe and go on my merry way. Later, bro," the man in the stall said.

Scott couldn't urinate because he was too distracted by the loud conversation. The man eventually came out of the stall and walked out without washing his hands. He didn't leave a tip. As he exited the room, Chuck entered it. He used the urinal next to Scott.

"Looks like we're on the same schedule, you son of a bitch," Chuck said.

"Yeah, guess so," Scott said in an annoyed tone.

"So, lemme see what you're packing," Chuck said as he looked over the partition between the urinals.

"What? What are you doing?" Scott said as he jerked his waist away from Chuck's direction.

"Just yankin' yer dick, that's all."

"What?"

"Relax. It's just an expression, Scott. I'm not really going to tug your penis. Where are you from, anyway? You seem like you may have grown up in the suburbs."

"I grew up in Chicago. I can't concentrate when someone's talking to me."

"Can't concentrate when someone's talking to you? What do you mean? That means you're unable to have a conversation."

"I don't mean in conversation. I mean while using the restroom."

"Oh. I dictate notes to my secretary while I'm taking a shit. I usually joke with her by farting at the points where I want my periods to be. Like, I'll say 'It was a pleasure to do business with you,' and then I'll fart. That's when Maxine knows to add a period."

"Oh."

"Yeah, well, whatever. I'll let you get back to business," Chuck said as he flushed. He walked to the attendant and asked for his name. He proceeded to have a conversation with him.

This was all too distracting for Scott. He pretended to urinate, but didn't. He flushed and walked towards the sink. Chuck introduced him to the attendant.

"Raul, this here is my friend Scott. Scott, this here is Raul."

Scott smiled and put his hands in the sink.

"That's rude of you, boy, to not shake this man's hand after being introduced," Chuck said.

"I was just going to wash my hands," Scott explained.

"I don't care if you were about to feed a starving Ethiopian, you don't get introduced to someone and not shake his hand immediately. This man has been drying people's hands all night. Shake his fucking hand, you horse's cum."

Scott pulled his hands out of the sink and shook Raul's hand.

"I knew they taught manners in Chicago!" Chuck exclaimed. "How's your evening, Raul?"

"It's good," Raul replied.

"Good to know! Scott and I are here with our better halves. They're two beautiful women. Though, Scott's girl's got bigger cans, mine's got a cushier caboose."

Raul chuckled. Scott was uncomfortable again.

"Alright, Raul, you have yourself a good-night. The missus and I are heading out of here soon. Scott, I'll see you outside," Chuck said as he dropped a twenty-dollar bill into the tip basket and walked out.

Scott finished washing his hands, left a one-dollar tip, and walked out of the restroom to find Chuck standing just outside.

"You know, my uncle Frank was the first guy to ever hold a lighter up at a concert during a slow song. It was Dylan in sixty-four. It's done to death now, and not genuine at all," Chuck said.

"Uh, ok?" Scott responded.

"Don't believe me? Wikipedia, motherfucker."

"Oh, alright. I'll look into it."

"You won't be sorry. Step outside with me for a minute while I smoke a cigarette," Chuck prepositioned. "What's your brand of choice?"

"I don't smoke."

"Don't smoke? Listen, Scott, you're gonna die anyway. There's no need to think you're better than people who already know that. Smoke a fucking cigarette with me, you uneven-breasted hippie."

"Um, I think I'd rather not."

"Alright, suit yourself. I bet you're dying before I do, and I've been smoking for twenty-seven years. Come on, let's go out through the kitchen."

Chuck led Scott through the kitchen as if he knew where he was going and had taken that path at least a hundred times before.

They found themselves in the alleyway, next to the dumpster.

Chuck proceeded to smoke his Camel cigarette.

"So, Scott, when are you gonna put a ring on Betty's finger?"

"I get asked this at least once a week by my mother. I don't know. The thought of marriage is overwhelming."

"I'm married. I don't feel overwhelmed, and I make a lot of money."

"Yeah, well, I don't know."

"You want to be like that poor sap who was rejected by his girlfriend earlier? Eh, on second thought, maybe it's for the better. I sometimes wish I were single. The tools you guys have to get pussy these days are basically giving it to you on a platter. There are these fucking apps that deliver girls to your phone. Where the fuck was this when I was younger?"

"You won't even have to talk to people in order to meet them anymore," Scott said and chuckled. Chuck didn't reciprocate.

"That's not funny. The human race is going to shit. Anyway, you have a good girl by your side, and you didn't need a computer or an app to meet her. If she were internet dating, she'd be blowing up. How do you feel about married women? You think they lose their looks as soon as they leave the chapel, like a new car loses its value after it's driven off the lot?"

"What? Of course not!"

"You say that emphatically. I'm glad you think that. Which leaves me with my next question – have you and Betty ever considered swinging?"

"Swinging?"

"Yeah, swinging, you know, swapping women."

"No, why would we ever consider that?"

"You know, to have fun. Why else? Betty and I have worked together for a long time. There were times we spent late nights at the office. I'm not gonna lie to you and say there weren't times I thought about fucking her – I'm sorry, that was crass – I mean, doing her doggy-style over the conference room table."

An intense tingling sensation swarmed throughout Scott's body. His ears rang as if sirens were sounding off at every rooftop in town. He clenched his fists.

"How about I proposition this. Tonight, as we leave, you go to my place with Elizabeth. Don't worry, Chuck, Jr. is staying with his aunt tonight, so you've got the place to yourself. She likes you, I could tell. I'll take off with Betty, but as a sign of respect, I won't have my way with her at your apartment. That'd just be wrong. I'll take her to the Twin Palms motel, off Stanton. I won't soil your sheets. A man's bed is his castle. I'm getting a new bed delivered in a few days, so you could go to town on mine."

Scott couldn't believe what he was hearing. He didn't know how to respond without knocking Chuck's teeth out.

"Don't just stand there, say something. Gimme a resounding or a mild yes — anything but a no, because it would be magical to do this tonight."

Enraged, Scott shoved Chuck against the dumpster. He then kicked him on the right shin. When Chuck went down to rub it, Scott punched him across the face. As Chuck went down to the pavement, Scott kicked him repeatedly. He grabbed a lid from a nearby garbage can and began to repeatedly hit Chuck over the head with it.

"You act like an asshole the whole fucking night, and then have the balls to ask to fuck my girlfriend? Who the fuck do you think you are?" Scott repeated multiple times as he beat Chuck, causing him to bleed from his nose and mouth.

"But I said you could fuck my wife, too," Chuck said groggily.

That further enraged Scott.

"Just because you said I could fuck your wife, you think I'd let you fuck my girlfriend, you vile piece of shit?"

He kicked Chuck in the face for a full minute. Chuck was either unconscious or dead, Scott couldn't decide — but leaning towards unconscious. He grabbed Chuck off the ground and tossed him into the dumpster. When he turned to walk back through the kitchen, he saw two restaurant workers looking at him as they smoked cigarettes. Shocked, Scott didn't know what to do. In unison, both men shrugged their shoulders, flicked their cigarettes, and walked back inside the kitchen. Scott was surprised that he was able to get away with the beating. He walked inside the kitchen, towards the dining area, and came across the two men. One was simmering meat while the other was cutting a piece of chicken. One of the men looked at the other. They both stopped what they were doing and put their right fists out. Scott pounded both fists with his.

"A rat is a rat, but a man is a man," one of the men said.

Scott nodded his head to the both of them as if he knew what that meant and proceeded to the table.

"Where have you guys been? Where's Chuck?" Betty asked.

"Chuck and I were in the restroom. He said he needed to get cigarettes, but went out through the kitchen because he said he wanted to see the behind the scenes action going on in there. I'm not feeling very well at all. Honey, I think I have to go."

"That's classic Chuck!" Betty said. "Aw, that's terrible you're not feeling well. Is your stomach acting up again?"

Scott made a pouty face, and said in a baby voice, "Yes."

"Alright, I guess we should go. Elizabeth, please give our regards to Chuck for leaving early," Betty said. "Here, this should cover our portion." She handed Elizabeth a one hundred-dollar bill.

"Oh, please, I wouldn't think of accepting your money. Please, let us take care of it," Elizabeth said.

"No, no, I insist," Betty said.

"I wouldn't think of it!" Elizabeth responded.

"Alright, fair enough. You take care of the bill this time," Scott interrupted. "The next time we go out – and I do hope that's sometime soon – we'll take care of the tab. How does that sound to you two?"

Both women agreed.

"Great! I had such a fun time! Please tell Chuck that I'm very much looking forward to seeing him again," Scott said as he put his jacket on. "I hope you both have a wonderful evening."

### Table 5 – Alex, Jared, Lillia, Zoe

"I wanna go home, mom," Zoe said to her mother for the seventh time in thirty minutes.

"Honey, we're not finished with our meals yet," Zoe's mother, Lillia, said. "Jared, hon, will you please talk some sense to her?"

"Zoe, honey, we need you to play it cool. You're disturbing the mantra of the table. Remember what we taught you. Breathe in and be one with inanimate objects. Look at your brother. He looks like he's found zen," Jared, Zoe's father, said.

"Yeah, pop, I'm on a whole other level," Alex said as his legs were crossed on the chair. He soon uncrossed them and placed his feet in the bowl filled with tomato spinach soup he placed on the floor.

"You see, Zoe, you need to relax, ok?" Jared said.

"Dad, Alex is messing with you. He's splattering his feet, which are covered in soup, all over the crotch of your yoga pants. Why'd you leave them on the floor, anyway?"

Alex was leaving soupy footprints across the crotch of his father's pants left neatly folded on the floor by his chair.

"Not cool, Alex. Not...cool..." Jared said.

"Is that supposed to be funny, Alex?" Lillia asked. "Because if it is, I don't get it. Though, if I do get it, which I think I might, then I don't think it's funny."

"Loosen up, dudes, it'll come right off," Alex said.

"You know we're all about artistic expression, Alex, but you don't go around doing that to daddy's two hundred-dollar yoga pants. How am I supposed to get my groove on tomorrow now? I'm so angry that I've lost my appetite," Jared said. "Are you happy?"

"I am. Does that mean we could go now?" Zoe said.

"Hardy-har-har, Zoe. Now, that joke I get. Your father may be finished with his food, but I'm still waiting on dessert," Lillia said. "What's your hurry anyway?"

"I have plans in an hour."

"Oh, and what, may I ask, do you have planned?"

"Things, mom, things..."

"Now, you kids know your father and I respect your privacy, but sometimes we need to know you're safe when you go out. That's the only reason why I'm asking, honey," Lillia said.

"Just know I'm always safe, mom, because I've always got this around," Alex said as he took out a switchblade from his back pocket.

"Where on Earth did you get that, Alex? Hand that to me this instant," Jared said.

"Relax, dad, it's just a switchblade," Alex said.

"I know exactly what it is. Where'd you get it?"

"This new kid at school sold it to me. It only cost a measly ten bucks. Check this out," Alex said and began twirling the blade between his fingers. He accidentally poked himself on his right middle finger, causing it to slightly bleed.

"You hand me that switchblade this minute! Look at what you've done to your finger," Lillia said as she took the switchblade from him.

"Yeah, look at how much blood, mom," Alex said as he raised his middle finger at his mother.

"Hey, smart guy, are you being fresh with your mother by raising that finger at her?" Jared asked. "You kids are impossible today! First off, you broke that glass – which, by the way, is coming out of your allowance, Alex."

"That's bullshit, dad!" Alex retorted.

"Alex! You know your mom and I are all about you kids expressing yourselves however you want to, but you can't say stuff like that with aggression – which I felt when you said it," Jared said.

"Sorry, dad, I do believe this is bullshit," Alex said in a calmer tone.

"That's a little better, I suppose. Anyway, you're being disruptive to the aura. Let your mother enjoy her dessert in peace when it gets here. Why don't you two take a walk?"

"Finally…" Zoe said as she got her purse and made her way outside. Alex followed her.

Zoe sat on the sidewalk curb.

"Mom and dad are so weird," Zoe said.

"Tell me about it," Alex said as he wiped the soup off his bare feet.

Zoe took out a flask from her purse and took a sip from it.

"What's that?" Alex asked.

"It's whiskey. Straight-up whiskey. You want some?"

"Did I take a dump in the bathroom fifteen minutes ago?" Alex asked.

"I don't know what you mean. Is that a yes or a no?"

"Yes! The answer to both is yes!"

Zoe gave Alex the flask. He gulped the alcohol.

"Watch it! The last thing I need is mom smelling it on you," Zoe said. She took the flask away from him and put it back inside her purse.

"Relax, it's not the first time I had it," Alex said.

"You're only eleven years old. When have you ever tried whiskey before?"

"A couple of years ago when mom wasn't looking, I went into the laundry room and took a sip of it instead of brushing my teeth."

"What are you talking about?"

"It was in the laundry room, in the red container."

"Red container in the laundry room? Wisk? You drank Wisk? Like, the laundry detergent?"

"Isn't this the same thing?"

"No, you idiot, you drank *Wisk*, the laundry soap. This is *whiskey*. I'm surprised you're not dead after drinking that. Also, it doesn't clean your teeth. What the hell is wrong with you?"

"Whatever, can I have another sip?"

"No, you already took a big gulp."

"Aww, come on! I wanna take another sip! Come on, don't be like that!"

"No, I'm already like the world's worst sister for giving you a sip of it in the first place."

"No fair! This is no fair at all!"

"What do you know about fair?"

Zoe's cell phone rang. She answered.

"Hey. Yeah, I'm still here. My mom's waiting for her dessert. I'm in the parking lot with my brother. You are? Sure, come by, I'll be here," she said, and ended the call.

"Who was that?" Alex asked.

"Caroline. She's a block away. She's going to stop by. Wait here while I go tell mom and dad she's coming. Hopefully they'll let me go with her. Don't do anything stupid," Zoe said as she walked back inside the restaurant.

Alex noticed she left her purse on the ground. Looking at his surroundings to see if the coast was clear, he stuffed his hands in it and pulled out the flask. He began to drink out of it again, despite hating the taste. He held his breath as he drank. It was a trick his caretaker at an after-school program he attended two years prior taught him. He remembered his caretaker Charlie telling him and the other after-school children to hold their breaths and take giant gulps if they were ever in a situation where they needed to impress a girl with a drink that had a bad taste. He also told them it was cost-efficient to chug as many beers as possible minutes before any happy hour ended.

"Smell no stink, drink your drink," the phrase Charlie taught him, reverberated in Alex's mind as he chugged the whiskey in the flask.

Alex drank all of the whiskey. A car pulled up to the curb as he was putting the empty flask back into Zoe's purse.

"'Sup, Alex?" Caroline said from the driver's seat.

"Oh, hey, Caroline…" He said. His head felt like it was starting to swim.

"Where's your sister?"

"She's inside talking to my parents."

"Oh, cool..."

"Yeah, cool..."

They stood in silence for a full forty seconds before Zoe came outside.

"Hey, my mom's cool with me going with you," Zoe said to Caroline.

"Can I come?" Alex asked.

"Nope!" Zoe said.

"Why can't I go? Where are you going anyway?" Alex inquired.

"We're going to – wait, where *are* we going?" Zoe asked.

"You know that hot ponytailed guy who wears the banana in the cafeteria? I think he's a senior," Caroline said.

"Uh, Aarav Kappor? I'm in love with that guy," Zoe said.

"Yeah, him! Well, guess what he does."

"What?"

"He volunteers at the park, planting trees and baby bushes!"

"Get out of town! He just got so much hotter!"

"Well, he was doing that earlier. I just wanted you to know that he was a babe *and* eco-friendly. Get this – he's the bassist in a Ricky Rocket cover band, and they're playing a show at Voodoo Lounge in like an hour."

"Get out of here! I *love* Ricky Rocket, and Aarav's a bassist? Two dreams just coalesced into one – two stripes for my rainbow."

"That's one hot fucking rainbow!"

"Can I come?" Alex asked again. He was beginning to lose his balance.

"No. Let's go, Caroline. Alex, I'll see you later," Zoe said as she got in the car and drove off.

The whiskey was starting to take effect on Alex. He began doing roundhouse kicks, but felt his pants weren't allowing him to be very durable. He took them off. He thought he looked silly wearing a shirt in his underwear, so he took his shirt off as well. As he was roundhouse kicking, he knocked over a trash can by the restaurant entrance. He picked up a cigarette butt that spilled out of it and put it in back of his ear. He began to howl.

Talking to Alejandra at the front desk, Rafael heard the commotion outside. He looked out the window to see a boy in his underwear kicking plastic containers and chasing after pigeons.

"Hey, you crazy kid! Put some clothes on and stop doing that! What's a-matter with you?" Rafael yelled out the door.

Alex walked like a chimpanzee towards Rafael and howled in his face. Rafael swung an open palm, but Alex crouched and grabbed Rafael's crotch, and howled even louder, causing his voice to crack. Rafael fell to the ground, and Alex stormed into the restaurant. Confused by the situation, Alejandra stood motionless as Alex sprinted past her.

"This key lime pie is delicious!" Lillia said. "We should order another for the kids."

"What the fuck?" Jared said as he saw Alex run past the dining area. "Was that who I think it was?"

Lillia spit the piece of pie she was chewing out of her mouth and ran after her son. Jared cut a piece of the pie with his fork and tasted it before he got up to follow his wife.

Alex ran into the restroom.

"What's going on here? Who are you?" Raul, the restroom attendant, asked when he saw Alex.

Alex ran into the stall farthest away and locked himself inside. He thought it would be funny to crawl from the locked stall he was in to another, locking that stall, too, and then crawl into a third stall, and locking that one, as well. He thought it would cause chaos because no one would understand why there was no one inside any the locked stalls.

Raul was livid.

"You make a mockery of my workspace? Get outta there, you little brat, I know which stall you're in." He hadn't realized Alex had crawled into another stall.

Lillia and Jared got to the restroom, as did Rafael and Alejandra.

"Alex! Alex, honey, come out. We know you're in there," Lillia said.

"Mom, I want to go home," Alex responded.

"Come out and we'll go home, son," Jared said.

Nervously, Alex unlocked the stall door and walked out. Rafael limped towards him.

"You little pendejo, look what you did to Rafael! He's inna lotta pain! Are you his parents?" Rafael asked, looking at Lillia and Jared.

"Yes, we're his parents," Lillia responded.

"Then Rafael knows what you need to do," he said as he

unbuckled his belt and handed it to Jared.

"Excuse me, what are you doing?" Jared asked.

"You need to punish him. Look at what he did to Rafael. He made a mess outside, disturbed Rafael's valued customers. No one wants to see a little boy in his underwear running around!"

"Speak for yourself," Raul said. He quickly followed with, "Just kidding, just kidding!"

"Stay out of this, Raul," Rafael said.

"I don't appreciate you telling me what I should do with my son," Jared said. "My wife and I completely understand what he did, and we'll reprimand him according to how we see fit. It will not involve violence, and we will certainly not do it in public – especially in front of you."

"Rafael must be dreaming. This is too much of a mess. Everyone out. Get your son, and get out. Rafael never wants to see you again. You're banned forever."

Lillia held onto Alex's arm as they made their slow, embarrassing walk out of the restaurant.

Rafael led the single file, followed by Alex, Lillia, Jared, and Alejandra. Back in the restroom, Raul couldn't figure out why the stalls were locked even though no one was inside any of them.

"Why can't I figure this out? I have a Ph.D. from Yale. I should be able to figure this out," he said to himself.

Rafael led the family outside.

"You are never to come here again. If you do, Rafael is calling the police. Rafael would have never thought that a family on Rafael's turf would act in such a manner. Shame on you. Rafael hopes your son learns discipline. Without it, this is what it looks like," he said, pointing to the turned over trash can and litter on the ground. "Now, get off the premises immediately." He closed the door.

"Put your pants on now this instant," Lillia said to Alex as she picked up his pants from the ground and handed them to him.

"And while you're at it, put this on as well," Jared said as he handed Alex his shirt. "You're in huge trouble. You have no idea what's coming to you."

"And don't think we don't smell the alcohol on your breath. You've turned into such a monster!" Lillia said. "I know your sister had her hand in this. Just wait until she gets home."

"You know your mother and I don't believe in punishment,"

Jared said.

"It impedes growing and learning from your mistake," Lillia interjected.

"Exactly. Your mother and I see eye-to-eye on this. However, this outburst, coupled with the severe underage drinking, may make us rethink this. Do you agree, Lillia?"

"Yes, I do."

"You're going to start volunteering at the park. Your mother and I have been wanting you to do it, but figured you and your sister would protest. You'll be learning responsibility while creating life by planting new trees and baby bushes. That'll show Zoe for getting you drunk."

"No ifs, ands, or buts from you, young man!" Lillia said.

"Fine! I don't care. I just want go to home!" Alex said.

"Alright, I'll get the Prius," Jared said. "Oh, for crying out loud!"

"What happened, honey?" Lillia asked.

"I forgot my yoga pants in there..."

## Table 6 – Alejandra

"Why are they still standing there?" Rafael said to himself as he looked out the glass door. "Rafael told them to leave the premises! He's coming this way! What a dummy!"

Alejandra stood next to him, unsure of how the evening got so out of hand.

"No, no, we don't have it! We threw them out! Yes, just now! They're in the dumpster! No, you can't get them! Go ahead, then sue Rafael and see what happens!" He yelled as he locked the door. He turned to Alejandra. "Keep this door locked. Rafael has his final customers for the night. Today has been too crazy. There is a bad moon out, and Rafael does not like it one bit!"

Alejandra looked at her watch.

"I didn't take my break. Can I take it now?" She asked.

"There are only a few tables left. Why don't you get something to eat and then go home for the night? But before you do that, throw out those disgusting pants on the floor by table five."

She sighed as she bent down to pick up the stained pants from the floor.

"Excuse me, you work here, right?" A woman asked her.

"Yes. How may I help you?" Alejandra replied.

"Well, my husband stepped out to buy cigarettes a little while ago. It's getting late, and I have to go. Could you let him know that I left if he comes back looking for me? A taxi is waiting outside. My name is Elizabeth. His name is Chuck. Could you do me that favor?"

"Yes, I will tell Chuck you left."

"You're a doll, doll. Have a goodnight."

Alejandra continued to the dumpster in the alley. She heard a faint banging from the inside of it. Weary, she ran to the kitchen and told Julio, one of the cooks.

"It's probably a rat that got caught in there," he told her.

"In that case, I don't want to go back out there! Could you throw this out for me? Pretty please, Julio?"

"You're lucky you've got a beautiful face, or else I'd tell you to go fuck yourself through the ear."

"That's so nice of you to say. So, you'll do it?"

"Yeah, I'll take care of it," he said as he took the pants. He picked up a butcher knife and walked towards the back.

"Why are you taking a knife?" She asked.

"It might be a big rat..." He said with a smirk.

"You're so weird sometimes," she said as she picked up a plate of chicken Parmesan. She walked to the dining area and sat at a vacant table.

She had worked double shifts all week, and despite the restaurant closing early that day, it couldn't be any sooner for her. There were four other tables with patrons. As she ate, she looked at each table, trying to figure out what the stories were for each of the people seated at them. One table included a man and woman. She saw they both had wedding bands on their fingers, so she knew they were married – but was it to each other? The next table had two women seated at it. They looked like they could be in their late-twenties or early-thirties. They could be sisters, but there were discernable differences that didn't make them look as if they were related. She looked at the third table, an elderly couple. She noticed that the woman had bandages on her wrists. That was as far as she got thinking about them before she was interrupted.

"Did you take care of the pants?" Rafael asked.

"Yes, I did. They've been thrown away."

"Good. Raul needs help in the men's room. The stalls are locked, but there's nobody in them! Help him unlock the stalls. He's an old man, and cannot crawl as well as he used to."

"Does it have to be now? I'm in the middle of eating my meal."

"Rafael does not say what you should or should not do. However, Rafael will say that this will be remembered."

Alejandra put her fork and knife down, and walked into the men's restroom.

"You will not believe this! No one is inside these two stalls. No one! Yet, the doors are locked! That's impossible!" Raul said. "Could you crawl underneath and unlock them?"

"Sure, I mean, what else am I good for?" Alejandra said sarcastically.

She crawled underneath the stalls and unlocked each of the doors. She returned to her table to find her food had been taken away.

She sat and pulled out her cell phone to call her boyfriend, Nicholas. He didn't answer. She immediately received a text from him.

"Wat's up?" His text read.

"Why didn't you pick up your phone? And why are you texting me back after I called you?" She texted back.

"I dunno. Wat's up?"

"This is so annoying," she texted. She called him again. He didn't pick up.

"Problem? Saw u called again," he texted. She grew aggravated.

"Can you pick me up from work? I'm getting out early."

"Dunno. The game is about to start."

"It's not that far. Please pick me up." There was no response. "Hello?" She texted five minutes later.

"Sorry. National anthem was on," he replied. She felt the urge to throw her phone through the window.

"Can you please pick me up?"

"Ur so close. Take the bus."

"It'll only take you like ten minutes!"

"Sorry. Can't text. Game on."

She couldn't believe what she was reading. She sighed and put her phone in her pocket.

"Excuse me, is it ok if I sit here?" A man standing at the other end of the table asked, startling her.

She looked at him and realized he was the man sitting alone at the fourth occupied table.

"Sure, I suppose so…" She said.

"How's your evening?" He asked as he sat down in the empty chair.

"It's not bad. I'm a little tired. I've been working a lot lately."

"Yeah, same with me. I decided to treat myself by getting some fine dining on my own. I know it's usually seen as a weird thing."

"What's a weird thing?"

"Going to a restaurant by yourself. Ordering food for one. Drinking wine for one. It seems like it's rare to see people eating by themselves at any establishment that has waiters."

"I like doing things on my own. I go at my own pace, and no one bothers me," she said while accidentally making eye contact.

"Oh, I'm sorry, do you want to be alone? I'm sorry if I've interrupted."

"No, no. It's fine. I didn't mean to look directly at you when I said that. Seriously, it's fine. We're closing soon anyway."

"Really? It's only a little after eight o'clock. That's pretty early, isn't it?"

"It's been a very interesting day, to say the least. I think we've all had about enough of everything that's happened."

"Do you mean that kid running around in his underwear? You're closing because of that? I thought that was hilarious."

"Well, there have been other things going on tonight, believe it or not."

"Really? That's interesting. If it deals with something personal, I'll understand if you don't want to get into it."

"It's nothing serious. It's just been a strange day, that's all."

"Oh, ok. Well, that makes your job more interesting, I suppose. Do you live close to here?"

"Not too far, only about a ten-minute drive."

"Oh, not a far commute at all. It must be nice to live so close to work."

"Not really," she said and laughed. He laughed with her.

"Yeah, I get it. I'd hate living so close to work, too," he said.

"It's not always good to live close to work. I used to live across the street from my elementary school, so I had no excuse for ever being late."

"That's the worst. I lived across the street from the house I'd burglarize on a regular basis, so it was no fun for my neighbors."

"What?"

"It was a joke. A joke, I wasn't serious. I guess I shouldn't make jokes like that when I first meet someone. Say, I heard Tom Cruise ate here once. Is that true?" He said, quickly changing the subject.

"Yes, that's true. There's a picture of him by the entrance standing with some of the waiters."

"Oh, cool. I'll have to check that out. Did you meet him?"

"No, he came in on my day off. I missed him."

"That's unfortunate."

"Story of my life."

"What is, always missing Tom Cruise encounters?"

"Exactly."

"That's pretty funny. I could see why he came here. The chicken Parmesan is fantastic. I just had it."

"I had a little of it tonight. It's what I usually eat on my break."

"Look, we already have something in common."

"Yeah, I guess."

"I'm so stupid. I didn't even introduce myself. My name's Evan."

"Hello, Evan, my name is Alejandra."

"What a pretty name."

"Thank you."

"Do you have a boyfriend, Alejandra?"

"Yes, I do."

"He's a very lucky guy. I hope he treats you like a queen."

"Sometimes."

"Sometimes? That's unfortunate."

"Eh, I get used to it."

"Not all of us could be on our A-game all the time, I suppose."

"I guess so."

"So, what do you have planned after work? You have more time than usual to enjoy the evening."

"I'm just going to go home. I have to catch the bus soon, actually."

"Why doesn't your boyfriend pick you up?"

"He's at home watching some game."

"So? I don't know what that has to do with picking you up."

"I'm asking myself the same question."

"You deserve better than that, Alejandra."

"Thank you," she said as she blushed.

"A beautiful woman like yourself shouldn't have to take the bus."

"Why? Is someone going to kidnap me?"

"Let's hope not! I thought about doing it, but I thought it'd be better to control myself and not act upon it."

There was an awkward silence.

"There I go again with my weird jokes," he said.

"Yeah, but at least you have a sense of humor," she said as she got a text. It was from Nicholas.

"Bring 6 pack when u come home. Hurry," he texted.

She sighed and put the phone back in her pocket.

"Is everything ok?" Evan asked.

"Yeah, it's nothing," she said. She looked like she was going to cry.

"Are you ok?"

"Yeah, I'm fine. I should get going."

"This may sound weird, and I'm not trying to be forward, but do you need a lift somewhere? I have a car."

"That's so sweet of you to offer. Thank you, but I think I'll take the bus."

"Alright, I'll only ask once. I don't want to make you any more uncomfortable than I've already made you."

"Thank you. Well, have a good night," she said as she stood up.

"You, too. I've been meaning to tell you something."

"What?"

"I'm in love with you."

"What?"

"I know that sounds weird, but hear me out. I could tell a piece of both of our futures right now. Would you care to take a glimpse at it? It'll be quick, and then you could go on your way."

"That is weird, but why not? This day has been weird enough, why not take a stroll through my future?" She said and sat down again.

"Alright. Well, what's going to happen is that we're going to exchange contact information, and then I'll call you in a few days — most likely two. We're going to talk, I'll make you laugh, you'll make me laugh, and we'll have a very good conversation. You'll go back and forth about it in your head because you'll feel guilty. You won't know how you feel about your boyfriend and then me. You'll hate yourself because you had such a great conversation with me and realized that I made you laugh and feel a way your boyfriend hasn't in years. You'll feel awful that you were placed in the situation in the first place. You'll resent me for putting you in this situation you hate, and will often reference this conversation. You'll eventually go on a break or break-up with your boyfriend because of the way he neglects you, and because of the way you and I can communicate to each other. You'll be in a weird limbo state for a few weeks – maybe months – but then one of us will reach out to the other, and we'll both be reminded about how well we got along right now. During that conversation, we'll agree to go on a date. We'll do something fun like kayaking, go to the museum, or spelunking if that's your thing. That evening, we'll go to a restaurant. It likely won't be this place because I'm fairly confident you're sick of the food and people here. We'll go on a second date about a week or a week and a half after our first. We'll develop an even deeper connection during that time period. I will admit, though, that I'm not perfect and could be somewhat of an asshole at times. Eventually, somewhere down the line, I'll break your heart and will make you hate me. We'll both likely have thoughts about cheating on each other, and I'll probably yell at you and humiliate you in front of your friends and coworkers out of a blindly drunken rage one night after I get let go of my job or if something just doesn't go my way – which won't be your fault at all, but I'll likely yell at you anyway – and I apologize in advance for that misdirected anger. Know that I'll love you, despite my flaws and your own – which I'll eventually discover. No one is perfect. I'll make you doubt yourself and sink your self-esteem to an abysmal, earth-shattering low. We'll most likely get married one day, have two children, and live somewhere in Brooklyn. Our marriage will be sort of similar to when we were in the relationship – you'll hate me sometimes, but you'll also love me and wouldn't be able to imagine a life without me, and I with you. While we're married, you'll be tempted to cheat on me again, but I can't tell whether you'll go through with it. You'll start thinking about your current, but soon-to-be-ex-boyfriend, and wonder what he's doing at that time period in his life; whether you made the right decision; whether you're happy with me; and possibly curse this night because it's when we met.

Throughout our time together, I'll make your life a personal hell – while also making it a rapturous one. Our marriage bond will be so strong that we'll overcome our nuances and learn to be happy with each other – but without ever being complacent. We'll reach a compromise. But, it all starts now, right here, at this table, on this spot, as I speak this sentence. This is the rest of your life. You see me now as a stranger, but you'll love me as I am. I'm going to want to stuff you in the trunk of my car and drive it off a cliff at times, but I won't do that because you will eventually mean the world to me. Our two boys, by the way, will be good kids – though one will be uglier than the other, unfortunately."

Alejandra sat motionless and silent in her seat, locked into Evan's eyes.

"Well.... In that case.... How will it all end?" She asked.

"I can't foresee *that* far into our future, so we'll have to deal with it then."

"What's your name again?"

"Evan."

"Oh."

"Just wanted to let you know what you were getting yourself into. Do you want to go ahead with this?"

"Walk me to the bus stop."

Alejandra led him towards the front entrance.

"Rafael, I'm going home for the night," she yelled in a stoic tone towards the kitchen as the door closed behind the two of them.

## ABOUT THE AUTHOR

Freddie Zamora is a tall man who thoroughly enjoys observing unusual characters lurking in supermarkets at 3 a.m.; accompanying friends on Craigslist runs to pick up stuff like espresso machines, uneven shelves, novelty Blondie posters, etc.; cheese fries from diners; and three-way calls. He was born, raised, and currently lives in Queens, NY.